CABLE

Cable stood over Dancey with the Walker Colt in his hand. It was cocked and pointing directly at Dancey's head. Joe Bob and Royce said nothing.

Dancey said, "You're not proving anything with that gun in your hand."

"I don't have anything to prove."

Royce said, "You think we won't be back?"

Cable's gaze shifted. "You'll ride into a double load of buckshot if you do."

Royce seemed to grin. "Man, you're made to order. Duane's going to have some fun with you."

Dancey's eyes held on Cable. "So one man's going to stand us off."

"That's all it's taken so far."

LAST STAND AT SABER RIVER

LAST STAND
AT
SABER RIVER

Elmore Leonard

BANTAM BOOKS
TORONTO · NEW YORK · LONDON

*This low-priced Bantam Book
has been completely reset in a type face
designed for easy reading, and was printed
from new plates. It contains the complete
text of the original hard-cover edition.*
NOT ONE WORD HAS BEEN OMITTED.

LAST STAND AT SABER RIVER

*A Bantam Book / published by arrangement with the author
Bantam edition / September 1980*

ISBN 0-553-13696-8

Published simultaneously in the United States and Canada

*Bantam Books are published by Bantam Books, Inc. Its trade-
mark, consisting of the words "Bantam Books" and the por-
trayal of a bantam, is Registered in U.S. Patent and Trademark
Office and in other countries. Marca Registrada. Bantam
Books, Inc., 666 Fifth Avenue, New York, New York 10103.*

PRINTED IN THE UNITED STATES OF AMERICA

0 9 8 7 6 5 4 3 2 1

Chapter One

Paul Cable sat hunched forward at the edge of the pine shade, his boots crossed and his elbows supported on his knees. He put the field glasses to his eyes again and, four hundred yards down the slope, the two-story adobe was brought suddenly, silently before him.

This was The Store. It was Denaman's. It was a plain, tan-pink southern Arizona adobe with a wooden loading platform, but no *ramada* to hold off the sun. It was the only general supply store from Hidalgo north to Fort Buchanan; and until the outbreak of the war it had been a Hatch & Hodges swing station.

The store was familiar and it was good to see, because it meant Cable and his family were almost home. Martha was next to him, the children were close by; they were anxious to be home after two and a half years away from it. But the sight of a man Cable had never seen before—a man with one arm—had stopped them.

He stood on the loading platform facing the empty sunlight of the yard, staring at the willow trees that screened the river close beyond the adobe, his right hand on his hip, his left sleeve tucked smoothly, tightly into his waist. Above him, the faded, red-lettered *Denaman's Store* inscription extended the full width of the adobe's double doors.

Cable studied the man. There was something about him.

Perhaps because he had only one arm. No, Cable thought then, that made you think of the war, the two and

1

a half years of it, but you felt something before you saw he had only one arm.

Then he realized it was the habit of surviving formed during two and a half years of war. The habit of not trusting any movement he could not immediately identify. The habit of not walking into anything blindly. He had learned to use patience and weigh alternatives and to be sure of a situation before he acted. As sure as he could be in his own mind.

Now Cable's glasses moved over the wind-scarred face of the adobe, following the one-armed man's gaze to the grove of willows and the river hidden beyond the hanging screen of branches.

A girl came out of the trees carrying a bucket and Cable said, "There's Luz again. Here—" He handed the glasses to his wife who was kneeling, sitting back on her legs, one hand raised to shield her eyes from the sun glare.

Martha Cable raised the glasses. After a moment she said, "It's Luz Acaso. But still it doesn't seem like Luz."

"All of a sudden she's a grown-up woman," Cable said. "She'd be eighteen now."

"No," Martha said. "It's something else. Her expression. The way she moves."

Through the glasses, the girl crossed the yard leisurely. Her eyes were lowered and did not rise until she reached the platform and started up the steps. When she looked up her face was solemn and warm brown in the sunlight. Martha remembered Luz's knowing eyes and her lips that were always softly parted, ready to smile or break into laughter. But now she wore an expression of weariness. Her eyes went to the man on the platform, then away from him quickly as he glanced at her and she passed into the store.

She's tired, or ill, Martha thought. Or afraid.

"She went inside?" Cable asked.

The glasses lowered briefly and Martha nodded. "But he's still there. Cable, for some reason I think she's afraid of him."

"Maybe." He watched Martha concentrating on the man on the platform. "But why, if Denaman's there?"

"If he's there," Martha said.

"Where else would he be?"

2

"I was going to ask the same question."

"Well, let's take it for granted he's inside."

"And Manuel?" She was referring to Luz's brother.

"Manuel could be anywhere."

Martha was still watching the man on the platform, studying him so that an impression of him would be left in her mind. He was a tall man, heavy boned, somewhat thin with dark hair and mustache. He was perhaps in his late thirties. His left arm was off between the shoulder and the elbow.

"I suppose he was in the war," Martha said.

"Probably." Cable nodded thoughtfully. "But which side?" That's something, Cable said to himself. You don't trust him. Any man seen from a distance you dislike and distrust. It's good to be careful, but you could be carrying it too far.

Briefly he thought of John Denaman, the man who had given him his start ten years before and talked him into settling in the Saber River valley. It would be good to see John again. And it would be good to see Luz, to talk to her, and Manuel. His good friend Manuel. Luz and Manuel's father had worked for Denaman until a sudden illness took his life. After that, John raised both of them as if they were his own children.

"Now he's going inside," Martha said.

Cable waited. After a moment he turned, pushing himself up, and saw his daughter standing only a few feet away. Clare was six, their oldest child: a quiet little girl with her mother's dark hair and eyes and showing signs of developing her mother's clean-lined, easily remembered features; resembling her mother just as the boys favored their father. She stood uncertainly with her hands clutched to her chest.

"Sister, you round up the boys."

"Are we going now?"

"In a minute."

He watched her run back into the trees and in a moment he heard a boy's shrill voice. That would be Davis, five years old. Sandy, not yet four, would be close behind his brother, following every move Davis made; almost every move.

Cable brought his sorrel gelding out of the trees and

3

stepped into the saddle. "He'll come out again when he hears me," Cable said. "But wait till you see us talking before you come down. All right?"

Martha nodded. She smiled faintly, saying, "He'll probably turn out to be an old friend of John Denaman's."

"Probably."

Cable nudged the sorrel with his heels and rode off down the yellow sweep of hillside, sitting erect and tight to the saddle with his right knee touching the stock of a Spencer carbine, his right elbow feeling the Walker Colt on his hip, and keeping his eyes on the adobe now, thinking: This could be a scout. This could be the two and a half years still going on. . . .

As soon as he had made up his mind to enlist he had sold his stock, all of his cattle, all two hundred and fifty head, and all but three of his horses. He had put Martha and the children in the wagon and taken them to Sudan, Texas, to the home of Martha's parents. He did this because he believed deeply in the Confederacy, as he believed in his friends who had gone to fight for it.

Because of a principle he traveled from the Saber River, Arizona Territory, to Chattanooga, Tennessee, taking with him a shotgun, a revolving pistol and two horses; and there on June 21, 1862, he joined J. A. Wharton's 8th Texas Cavalry, part of Nathan Bedford Forrest's command.

Three weeks later Cable saw his first action and received his first wound during Forrest's raid on Murfreesboro. On September 3, Paul Cable was commissioned a captain and appointed to General Forrest's escort. From private to captain in less than three months; those things happened in Forrest's command. Wounded twice again after Murfreesboro; the third and final time on November 28, 1864, at a place called Huey's Mills—shot from his saddle as they crossed the Duck River to push Wilson's Union Cavalry back to Franklin, Tennessee. Cable, with gunshot wounds in his left hip and thigh, was taken to the hospital at Columbia. On December 8 he was told to go home "the best way you know how." There were more seriously wounded men who needed his cot; there would be a flood of them soon, with General Hood about to

4

pounce on the Yankees at Nashville. Go home, he was told, and thank God for your gunshot wounds.

So for Cable the war was over, though it was still going on in the east and the feeling of it was still with him. He was not yet thirty, a lean-faced man above average height and appearing older after his service with Nathan Bedford Forrest: after Chickamauga, had come Fort Pillow, Bryce's Crossroads, Thompson's Station, three raids into West Tennessee and a hundred nameless skirmishes. He was a calm-appearing man and the war had not changed that. A clear-thinking kind of man who had taught himself to read and write, taught himself the basic rules and his wife had helped him from there.

Martha Sanford Cable was twenty-seven now. A West Texas girl, though convent-educated in New Orleans. Seven years before she had left Sudan to come to the Saber River as Paul Cable's wife, to help him build a home and provide him with a family. . . .

Now they were returning to the home they had built with the family they had begun. They were before Denaman's Store, only four miles from their own land.

And Cable was entering the yard, still with his eyes on the loading platform and the double doors framed in the pale wall of the adobe, reining in his sorrel and approaching at a walk.

The right-hand door opened and the man with one arm stepped out to the platform. He walked to the edge of it and stood with his thumb in his belt looking down at Cable.

Cable came on. He kept his eyes on the man, but said nothing until he had pulled to a halt less than ten feet away. From the saddle, Cable's eyes were even with the man's knees.

"John Denaman inside?"

The man's expression did not change. "He's not here any more."

"He moved?"

"You could say that."

"Maybe I should talk to Luz," Cable said.

The man's sunken cheeks and the full mustache covering the line of his mouth gave his face a hard, bony expression, but it was not tensed. He said, "You know Luz?"

5

"Since she was eight years old," Cable answered. "Since the day I first set foot in this valley."

"Well, now—" The hint of a smile altered the man's gaunt expression. "You wouldn't be Cable, would you?"

Cable nodded.

"Home from the wars." The man still seemed to be smiling. "Luz's mentioned you and your family. Her brother too. He tells how you and him fought off Apaches when they raided your stock."

Cable nodded. "Where's Manuel now?"

"Off somewhere." The man paused. "You been to your place yet?"

"We're on our way."

"You've got a surprise coming."

Cable watched him, showing little curiosity. "What does that mean?"

"You'll find out."

"I think you're changing the subject," Cable said mildly. "I asked you what happened to John Denaman."

For a moment the man said nothing. He turned then and called through the open door, "Luz, come out here!"

Cable watched him. He saw the man's heavy-boned face turn to look down at him again, and almost immediately the Mexican girl appeared in the doorway. Cable's hand went to the curled brim of his hat.

"Luz, honey, you're a welcome sight." He said it warmly, and he wanted to jump up on the platform and kiss her but the presence of this man stopped him.

"Paul—"

He saw the surprise in the expression of her mouth and in her eyes, but it was momentary and she returned his gaze with a smile that was grave and without joy, a smile that vanished the instant the man with one arm spoke.

"Luz, tell him what happened to Denaman."

"You haven't told him?" She looked at Cable quickly, then seemed to hesitate. "Paul, he's dead. He died almost a year ago."

"Nine months," the man with one arm said. "I came here the end of August. He died the month before."

Cable's eyes were on the man, staring at him, feeling now that he had known Denaman was dead, had sensed it from the way the man had spoken—from the tone of his voice.

"You could have come right out and told me," Cable said.

"Well, you know now."

"Like you were making a game out of it."

The man stared down at Cable indifferently. "Why don't you just let it go?"

"Paul," Luz said, "it came unexpectedly. He wasn't sick."

"His heart?"

Luz nodded. "He collapsed shortly after noon and by that evening he was dead."

"And you happened to come a month later," Cable said, looking at the man again.

"Why don't you ask what I'm doing here?" The man looked up at the sound of the double team wagon on the grade, his eyes half closed in the sunlight, his gaze holding on the far slope now. "That your family?"

"Wife and three youngsters," Cable said.

The man's gaze came down. "You made a long trip for nothing." He seemed about to smile, though he was not smiling now.

"All right," Cable said. "Why?"

"Some men are living in your house."

"If there are, they're about to move."

The smile never came, but the man stared down at Cable intently. "Come inside and I'll tell you about it." Then he turned abruptly, though he glanced again at the approaching wagon before going into the store.

Cable could hear the jingling, creaking sound of the wagon closer now, but he kept his eyes on Luz until she looked at him.

"Luz, who is he?"

"His name is Edward Janroe."

"The man acts like he owns the place."

Her eyes rose briefly. "He does. Half of it."

"But why—"

"Are you coming?" Janroe was in the doorway. He was looking at Cable and with a nod of his head indicated Luz. "You got to drag things out of her. I've found it's more trouble than it's worth." He waited until Cable stirred in the saddle and began to dismount. "I'll be inside," he said, and stepped away from the door.

Cable dropped his reins, letting them trail. He swung down and mounted the steps to the platform. For a moment he watched Luz Acaso in silence.

"Are you married to him?"

"No."

"But he's been living here eight months and has a half interest in the store."

"You think what you like."

"I'm not thinking anything. I want to know what's going on."

"He'll tell you whatever you want to know."

"Luz, do you think I'm being nosy? I want to help you."

"I don't need help." She was looking beyond him, watching the wagon entering the yard.

All right, he thought, don't push her. It occurred to him then that Martha was the one to handle Luz. Why keep harping at her and get her nervous. Martha could soothe the details out of her in a matter of minutes.

Cable patted her shoulder and stepped past her into the abrupt dimness of the store.

He moved down the counter that lined the front wall, his hand gliding along the worn, shiny edge of it and his eyes roaming over the almost bare shelves. There were scattered rows of canned goods, bolts of material, work clothes, boxes that told nothing of their contents. Above, Rochester lamps hanging from a wooden beam, buckets and bridles and coils of rope. Most of the goods on the shelves had the appearance of age, as if they had been here a long time.

Cable's eyes lowered and he almost stopped, unexpectedly seeing Janroe beyond the end of the counter in the doorway to the next room. Janroe was watching him closely.

"You walk all right," Janroe said mildly. "Not a mark on you that shows; but they wouldn't have let you go without a wound."

"It shows if I walk far enough," Cable said. "Or if I stay mounted too long."

"That sounds like the kind of wound to have. Where'd you get it?"

"On the way to Nashville."

"With Hood?"

"In front of him. With Forrest."

"You're a lucky man. I mean to be in one piece."

"I suppose."

"Take another case. I was with Kirby Smith from the summer of sixty-one to a year later when we marched up the Kentucky River toward Lexington. Near Richmond we met a Yankee general named Bull Nelson." Janore's eyes narrowed and he grinned faintly, remembering the time. "He just had recruits, a pick-up army, and I'll tell you we met them good. Cut clean the hell through them, and the ones we didn't kill ran like you never saw men run in your life. The cavalry people mopped up after that and we took over four thousand prisoners that one afternoon."

Janroe paused and the tone of his voice dropped. "But there was one battery of theirs on a ridge behind a stone fence. I was taking some men up there to get them . . . and the next day I woke up in a Richmond field hospital without an arm."

He was watching Cable closely. "You see what I mean? We'd licked them. The fight was over and put away. But because of this one battery not knowing enough to give up, or too scared to, I lost a good arm."

But you've got one left and you're out of the war, so why don't you forget about it, Cable thought, and almost said it; but instead he nodded, looking at the shelves.

"Maybe Luz told you I was in the army," Janroe said.

"No, only your name, and that you own part of the store."

"That's a start. What else do you want to know?"

"Why you're here."

"You just said it. Because I own part of the store."

"Then how you came to be here."

"You've got a suspicious mind."

"Look," Cable said quietly, "John Denaman was a friend of mind. He dies suddenly and you arrive to buy in."

9

"That's right. But you want to know what killed him?"

When Cable said nothing Janroe's eyes lifted to the almost bare shelves. "He didn't have enough goods to sell. He didn't have regular money coming in. He worried, not knowing what was going to happen to his business." Janroe's gaze lowered to Cable again. "He even worried about Luz and Vern Kidston. They were keeping company and, I'm told, the old man didn't see eye to eye with Vern. Because of different politics, you might say. So it was a combination of things that killed him. Worries along with old age. And if you think it was anything else, you're going on pure imagination."

"Let's go back to Vern Kidston," Cable said. "I never heard of him; so what you're saying doesn't mean a whole lot."

Janroe's faint smile appeared. "Vern came along about two years ago, I'm told. He makes his living supplying the Union cavalry with remounts. Delivers them up to Fort Buchanan."

"He lives near here?"

"In the old Toyopa place. How far's that from you?"

"About six miles."

"They say Vern's fixed it up."

"It'd take a lot of fixing. The house was half burned down."

"Vern's got the men."

"I'll have to meet him."

"You will. You'll meet him all right."

Cable's eyes held on Janroe. "It sounds like you can hardly wait."

"There's your suspicious mind again." Janroe straightened and stepped into the next room. "Come on. It's time I poured you a drink."

Cable followed, his gaze going from left to right around the well-remembered room: from the door that led to the kitchen to the roll-top desk to the Hatch & Hodges calendar to the corner fireplace and the leather-bottomed chairs, to the pictures of the Holy Family and the Sierra Madre landscapes on the wall, to the stairway leading to the second floor (four rooms up, Cable remembered), and finally to the round dining table between the front windows. He watched Janroe go into the kitchen and come out with a bottle of mescal and two glasses, holding the glasses in his fingers and the bottle pressed between his arm and his body.

Janroe nodded to the table. "Sit down. You're going to need this."

Cable pulled out a chair and stepped over it. He watched Janroe sit down and pour the clear, colorless liquor.

"Does my needing this have to do with Vern Kidston?"

Janroe sipped his mescal and put his glass down gently. "Vern's the one living in your house. Not Vern himself. Some of his men." Janroe leaned closer as if to absorb a reaction from Cable. "They're living in your house with part of Vern's horse herd grazing in your meadow."

"Well"—Cable raised the glass of mescal, studying it in the light of the window behind Janroe—"I don't blame him. It's good graze." He drank off some of the sweet-tasting liquor. "But now he'll move his men out. That's all."

"You think so?"

"If he doesn't vacate I'll get the law."

"What law?"

"Fort Buchanan. That's closest."

"And who do you think the Yankees would side with," Janroe asked, "the ex-Rebel or the mustanger supplying them with remounts?"

Janroe looked up and Cable turned in his chair as Luz entered from the store. Behind her came Martha holding Sandy's hand and moving Clare and Davis along in front of her.

"We'll see what happens," Cable said. He rose, holding out his hand as Davis ran to him and stood close against his leg.

"Mr. Janroe, this is my wife, Martha." He glanced at Janroe who had made no move to rise. "This boy here is Davis. The little one's Sanford and our big girl there is Clare, almost seven years old already." Cable winked at his daughter, but she was staring with open curiosity at Janroe's empty sleeve.

Martha's hand went to the little girl's shoulder and

she smiled pleasantly at the man still hunched over the table.

"Mr. Janroe"—Martha spoke calmly—"you don't know how good it is to be back here again." She was worried one of the children might ask about Janroe's missing arm. Cable knew this. He could sense it watching her, though outwardly Martha was at ease.

Luz said, "I invited them for dinner."

Janroe was staring at Clare. She looked away and his eyes went to Davis, holding him, as if defying him to speak. Then, slowly, he sat back and looked up at Luz.

"Take the kids with you. They'll eat in the kitchen."

Luz hesitated, then nodded quickly and held out her hand to Sandy. The boy looked up at her and pressed closer into his mother's skirts.

"They're used to being with me," Martha said pleasantly. Gently she urged Clare forward, smiling at Luz now, though the Mexican woman did not return her smile. "While Cabe . . . while Paul was away the children didn't have the opportunity to meet many new people. I'm afraid they're just a little bit strange now."

"If they eat," Janroe said, "they still eat in the kitchen."

Martha's face colored. "Mr. Janroe, I was merely explaining—"

"The point is, Mrs. Cable, there's nothing to explain. In this house kids don't sit at the table with grownups."

Martha felt the heat on her face and she glanced at her husband, at Cable who stood relaxed with the calm, tell-nothing expression she had learned to understand and respect. It isn't your place to answer him, she thought. But now the impulse was too strong and she could no longer hold back her words, though when she spoke her voice was calm and controlled.

"Now that you've said it three times, Mr. Janroe, we will always remember that in this house children do not eat with grownups."

"Mrs. Cable"—Janroe spoke quietly, sitting straight up and with his hand flat and unmoving on the table—"if your husband has one friend around here it's going to be me. Not because I'm pro-South or anti-Union. Not because I favor the man who's at a disadvantage. But because I don't have a reason not to befriend your husband. Now that's a pretty flimsy basis for a friendship."

"If you think I was rude," Martha said patiently, "I apologize. Perhaps I did—"

"Just wait a minute." Janroe brought up his hand to stop her. "I want you to realize something. I want you to understand that I don't have to smile at your husband for his business. If you don't trade with me you go to Fort Buchanan and that's a two-day trip. Add to that, I do business with the Kidstons. They buy most of the goods as fast as I receive them. And I'll tell you right now, once they learn I'm dealing with your husband they're going to come in here and yell for me to stop."

"Mr. Janroe—"

"But you know what I'll answer them? I'll tell them to go to Buchanan or hell with their business, either one. Because no man on earth comes into my house and tells me what I can do or what I can't do. Not Vern Kidston or his brother; not you or your husband here."

Janroe relaxed against the back of his chair. "That's how it is, Mrs. Cable. I'd suggest you think about it before you speak out the first thing that comes to your mind."

Again there was silence. Cable saw his wife tense, controlling herself with a fixed tightness about her nose and mouth. She stared at Janroe.

"Martha," Cable said mildly, "why don't you take the children to the kitchen? Maybe you could help Luz dish up." Martha looked at him, but said nothing. She held out her hand to Davis, gathered her children about her, and followed the girl to the kitchen.

"Your wife looks like a woman of strong character," Janroe said as Cable sat down again.

"She sticks up for what she believes."

"Yes," Janroe said. "A strong-minded woman. I noticed you *asked* her when you told her to go to the kitchen. You said, 'Why don't you take the children? . . .'"

Cable stared at him. "I think I said that."

"I've found," Janroe said, "it works a sight better to *tell* women what to do. Never *ask* them. Especially a wife. You were away for a while and your wife took on some independence. Well, now you're back I'd suggest you assume your place as head of the family."

13

Cable leaned forward, resting his arms on the edge of the table. "Mr. Janroe, I'd suggest you mind your own business."

"I'm giving you good advice, whether you know it or not."

"All I know about you so far," Cable said quietly, "is that you like to talk. I've got no reason to respect your advice. I've got no reason to respect you or anything about you."

He saw Janroe about to speak. "Now wait a minute. You gave my wife a lecture on what she was supposed to understand. I stood by and watched you insult her. But now I'll tell you this, Mr. Janroe: if you didn't have the misfortune of being one-armed you never would have said those things. You might be a strong-minded, hard-nosed individual who doesn't care what anybody thinks and who won't stand for any kind of dependence. You might even be a man to admire. But if you had had both your arms when you said those things, I'd have broken your jaw."

Janroe stared at Cable, his chest rising and falling with his breathing. He remained silent.

"I'm sorry I had to say that," Cable told him after a moment. "But now we know where we stand. You've got your ideas and I've got mine. If they cross, then I guess you and I aren't going to get along."

Janroe sipped his mescal, taking his time, and set the glass down gently. "You were with Bedford Forrest," he said then. "Were you an officer?"

"I reached captain."

"That speaks well of you, doesn't it—an officer with Forrest?"

"It depends from which side you view it."

"How long were you with him?"

"Since June, sixty-two."

"In the saddle most every day. Living outside and fighting—" Janroe's head nodded slowly. He raised the glass again. "You might be able to break my jaw at that."

"Maybe I shouldn't have said that."

"Don't back off. I'm being realistic, not apologizing. I'm saying you *might*."

Cable stared at him. "Maybe we should start all over again."

14

"No, I think we've come a long way in a short time."

"Except," Cable said, "you know more about me than I do about you."

"You don't have to know anything about me," Janroe said. "The Kidstons are your problem."

"I'll talk to them."

"But why should they talk to you?" Janroe watched him intently. "You're one man against, say, fifteen. You're an ex-Confederate in Union territory. The Kidstons themselves are Yankees. They sell most of their cattle and all of their horses to the Union army. Vern's brother Duane even held a command, but now he's back and he's brought the war with him. Has everybody calling him 'The Major' and he orders Vern's riders about like they were his personal cavalry." Janroe shook his head. "They don't have to listen to you."

Cable shrugged. "We'll see what happens."

"How do you eat?" Janroe asked. "That's your first problem."

"For now," Cable said, "I plan to buy provisions and maybe shoot something. Pretty soon I'll start buying stock and build my herd again."

"Buy it from where?"

"South. Luz's brother has friends in Sonora. I sold my stock to them when I enlisted on the agreement they'd sell back whatever I could buy when I came home."

"Manuel's down that way right now," Janroe said.

Cable's eyes raised. "When will he be back?"

"In a few days, I suppose. But your problem is now. I said before, some of Vern's men are living at your place."

"I'll have a talk with them," Cable said.

"One of them was here this morning. Bill Dancey." Janroe paused as Luz approached the table. She put plates in front of them and a serving dish of meat stew between them. Janroe asked her, "Where's his wife?"

"With the children." Luz served them as she spoke.

"Was Dancey here this morning?"

"I saw no one else."

"Who's up there with him?"

"I think Royce and the one named Joe Bob Dodd."

"Tell Mr. Cable about them."

Luz looked off, as if picturing them, before her eyes

15

lowered to Cable. "Bill Dancey is head. He is a large man and wears a beard and is perhaps ten years older than the others. This Royce and the one called Joe Bob look much alike with their thin faces and bodies and their hats worn straight and low over their eyes. They stand with their hands on their hips in a lazy fashion and say things to each other and laugh, though not genuinely. I think they are Texans."

"They are," Janroe said. "I'm not sure about Dancey. But it's said this Joe Bob and Royce, along with Joe Bob's two older brothers, that's Austin and Wynn, deserted from Sherrod Hunter's Texas Brigade when he came through here and Duane Kidston hired them. They say if Duane knew they'd been Rebel soldiers he'd have a fit." Janroe paused. "Royce and Joe Bob are the ones at your place. Austin and Wynn are probably at the main house."

Cable said, "You're telling me not to go home?"

"I'm telling you how it is. You do what you want."

"We'll leave as soon as we load up."

From the platform Janroe watched the wagon, with Cable's sorrel trailing, move off toward the willows. He watched intently, his right hand on the stump of his arm and massaging it gently, telling himself not to become excited or hasty or jump to conclusions.

But, my God, it was more than he could have hoped blind luck would provide—an ex-Rebel suddenly showing up here; coming home to find the Kidstons on his land.

He's your weapon, Janroe thought. Now it was right in front of him after months of waiting and watching and wondering how he could make it happen and never be suspected. If necessary he would even apologize to Martha for what he'd said. It had come out too quickly, that was all. He would smooth it over if he had to, because Cable's presence could be far more important than where kids ate, or if they ate at all, for that matter. He would have to watch himself and not let his mind clutch at petty things just to be tearing something apart.

But think it out carefully, he thought, now that there could be a way. Don't stumble; he's right here waiting, but you have to use him properly.

Cable—Janroe could feel the certainty of it inside of

him—was going to help him kill Vern and Duane Kidston. And then, thinking of Cable's wife, he decided that before it was all over, Cable would be as dead as the two men he would help kill.

Cable forded the river at the store and followed it north out into the open sunlight of the mile-wide valley, then gradually west, for the valley curved in that direction with the river following close along its left, or west, slope. The far side of the valley was rimmed by a low, curving line of hills. The near slope also rolled green-black with pines; but beyond these hills, chimneyed walls of sandstone towered silently against the sky. Beyond the rock country lay the Kidston place.

Sandy was asleep. Davis and Clare sat on the endgate, Davis holding the reins of the sorrel. And Martha sat with Cable, listening in silence as he told her everything Janroe had said about the Kidstons.

When he had finished, Martha said, "What if they won't leave, Cabe? The ones in our house."

"Let's wait and see."

"I mean with the children to think of."

"The children and a lot of things," Cable said.

They talked about Luz then. Even in the kitchen, Martha said, Luz had acted strangely: tense and almost reluctant to talk even about everyday things. She did tell that the store had been left to them, to Manuel and herself, in John Denaman's will; and they would stay here. The grave of their mother in a Sonora village was the only tie they had with their birthplace; the store had been their home for a dozen years. Luz had been only six, Manuel twelve, when their father came here to work for John Denaman. The next year their father died of a sickness and John Denaman had cared for them from that day on.

But she related little more about Edward Janroe than what she had told Cable—the man's name, the fact that he owned a half interest in the store and had been here eight or nine months.

But if business was so poor, Cable asked, why would Janroe want to buy into the store?

Because of Luz? Martha offered.

Perhaps. Luz was a good-looking girl. Janroe could easily be attracted to her.

But Martha was sure that Luz still liked Vern Kidston. Luz mentioned that she used to see Vern frequently; but that was before Janroe came. Something else to wonder about. Though Janroe himself was the big quesiton.

"What do you think of him?" Cable asked.

"All I'm sure of is that he has a low opinion of women," Martha said mildly, "judging from the lecture he gave me."

"He won't do that again," Cable said. "I talked to him."

Martha smiled. She moved closer to her husband and put her arm through his.

They rode in silence until they saw, through the willow and aspen along the river, horses grazing farther up the meadow. Martha handed her husband the field glasses and took the reins.

"About thirty, just mares and foals," Cable said after a moment. "And a man with them."

Martha kept the team moving. They were close to the base of the slope with the dark well of pines above them and the river close on their right. Their house was perhaps a quarter of a mile ahead, no more than that, set back a hundred feet from the river; but it was still out of sight, hidden by the pine stands that straggled down from the slope.

Through the glasses, Cable saw the rider come out of the trees on this side of the river. He noticed that the man was bearded and remembered Luz Acaso's description of the one named Bill Dancey: older by ten years than the other two; the one in charge.

"He must have seen us," Cable said. "He just crossed over."

"Waiting for us?" asked Martha.

"No, going for the house." He handed the glasses to Martha, feeling the children close behind him now.

Davis said, "Can I look?"

"Not right now." Cable half turned on the seat. "Listen, I want you children to stay right where you are. Even when we stop, stay there and don't jump off."

18

Clare's dark eyes were round and open wide. "Why?"

"Because we're not sure we're staying."

Cable looked at the boy again. "Davis, you hold on to Sandy. You won't let him jump out now, will you?"

The little boy shook his head solemnly. "No, sir."

Cable smiled at his children. His hand reached to the wagon bed, felt the short barrel of the Spencer carbine, then moved to the shotgun next to it and brought it out, placing it muzzle-down between them on the seat.

"Martha, this one's yours. Put your hand on it when I climb off, but don't lift it unless you see you have to."

He drew the Walker Colt from its holster, eased back the hammer, turned the cylinder carefully, feeling the oil-smoothness of the action, and lowered the hammer again on the empty chamber.

"There's the house," Martha said anxiously. "Part of it." She could see an adobe-colored shape through the pines close in front of them.

Then, coming out of the trees, the house was in full view: a one-story adobe with an addition made of pine logs, a shingled roof and a ramada that ran the length of the adobe section. Beyond, part of the barn could be seen.

Cable's eyes were on the bearded rider. He was near the house, still mounted but facing them now, watching them approach. A second man had come out of the house and stood near the mounted man.

"This is far enough," Cable said. They were less than fifty feet from the men now. As the wagon stopped a third man, thumbing a suspender strap up over his bare chest, appeared in the doorway of the adobe. All three men were armed. Even the one in the doorway, though half dressed, wore crossed belts holding two holstered revolvers.

"The one in the door," Cable said. "Keep a close eye on him." Martha made no answer, but he didn't look at her now. He breathed in and out slowly, calming himself and putting it off still another moment, before he jumped down from the wagon, holding his holster to his leg, and moved toward the mounted man.

"You were a while getting here," Bill Dancey said. He dismounted, swinging his leg over carefully, and stood with his feet apart watching Cable coming toward him.

Within two strides Cable stopped. "You knew we were coming?"

"Janroe mentioned it." Dancey's short-clipped beard hid any change of expression. He nodded toward the man who stood near him. "Royce here went in for something I forgot this morning and Janroe told him."

Cable glanced at the one called Royce: a tall, thin-framed man who stood hip-cocked with his thumbs hooked into his belt. His hat was tilted forward, low over his eyes, and he returned Cable's stare confidently.

Royce must have taken the horse trail, a shorter route that followed the crest of the slope, to and from the store; that's why they hadn't seen him, Cable decided.

He looked at Dancey again. "Did Janroe tell him it's my land you're on?"

Dancey nodded. "He mentioned it."

"Then I don't have to explain anything."

"That's right," Royce said. "All you have to do is turn around and go back."

There it was. Cable gave himself time, feeling the tension through his body and the anger, not building, but suddenly there as this lounging, lazy-eyed poser told him very calmly to turn around and go back. At least there was no decision to make. And arguing with him or with Dancey would only waste time. Even with Martha and the children here he knew how far he would go if necessary. He wanted to feel the anger inside of him because it would make it easier; but he wanted also to control it and he let his breath out slowly, shaking his head.

"I was afraid this was going to happen."

"Then why did you come?" Dancey asked.

The back of Cable's hand moved across his mouth, then dropped heavily. "Well, since I own this place—"

Dancey shook his head. "Vern Kidston owns it."

"Just took it?"

"In the name of the United States Government," Dancey said. "Mister, you must've been dreaming. You ever hear of Rebel land in Union territory?"

"I'm not a solider any more."

"You're not anything any more." Dancey glanced at the wagon. "Your wife's waiting for you. And the kids. You've got kids, haven't you?"

"Three."

"A man doesn't do anything crazy with three kids."

"Not very often," Cable said mildly. His eyes moved to Royce, then past him to the bare-chested man who had come out to the edge of the ramada shade. This would be Joe Bob Dodd. He stood with one hand on his hip, the other raised to a support post. He wore his hair with side-burns to the angle of his jaw. This and the dark line of hair down the bony whiteness of his chest made him appear obscenely naked. He was somewhat shorter than Royce but had the same slim-hipped, slightly stoop-shouldered build.

Cable's eyes returned to Dancey. "I'll give you the rest of the afternoon to collect your gear and clear out. Fair enough?"

Royce looked over at Joe Bob, grinning. "You hear what he said?"

The man at the ramada nodded. "I heard him."

"You don't have the time to give," Dancey said. "I told you, you're going to turn around and go back."

"Bill," Joe Bob called, "tell him he can leave his woman."

Cable's eyes went to him, feeling the tingle of anger again. No, wait a little more, he thought. Take one thing at a time and don't make it harder than it already is. His gaze returned to Dancey.

"Go get Kidston and I'll talk to him," Cable said.

"He wouldn't waste his time."

"Maybe I would though," Joe Bob said easily. His hand came down from the post and both thumbs hooked into his crossed belts. "Reb, you want to argue over your land?"

"I'll talk to Kidston."

"You'll talk to me if I say so."

Watching him, seeing him beyond the lowered head of Dancey's horse and feeling Dancey still close to him, Cable said, "I think that's all you are. Just talk."

"Bill," Joe Bob said, "get your horse out of the way."

Cable hesitated.

He sensed Dancey reaching for the reins, his body turning and his hands going to the horse's mane.

And for part of a moment Dancey was half turned

from him with his hands raised and the horse was moving, side-stepping, hiding both Royce and Joe Bob, and that was the time.

It was then or not at all and Cable stepped into Dancey, seeing the man's expression change to sudden surprise the moment before his fist hooked into the bearded face. Dancey stumbled against his horse, trying to catch himself against the nervously side-stepping animal, but Cable was with him, clubbing him with both fists, again and again and again, until Dancey sagged, until he went down covering his head.

Cable glanced at the wagon and away from it with the sound of Martha's voice and with the sound of running steps on the hard-packed ground. He saw Joe Bob beyond Dancey's horse. Now a glimpse of Royce jerking the bridle, and a slapping sound and the horse bolted.

Both Joe Bob and Royce stood in front of him, their hands on their revolvers; though neither of them had pulled one clear of its holster. They stood rooted, staring at Cable, stopped suddenly in the act of rushing him. For in one brief moment, in the time it had taken Royce to slap the horse out of the way, they had missed their chance.

Cable stood over Dancey with the Walker Colt in his hand. It was cocked and pointing directly at Dancey's head. Joe Bob and Royce said nothing. Dancey had raised himself on an elbow and was staring at Cable dumbly.

"Now you take off your belts," Cable said. He brought Dancey to his feet and had to prompt them again before they unbuckled their gun belts and let them fall. Then he moved toward Joe Bob.

"You said something about my wife."

"Me?"

"About leaving her here."

Joe Bob shrugged. "That wasn't anything. Just something I felt like saying—"

Abruptly Cable stepped into Joe Bob, hitting him in the face before he could bring up his hands. Joe Bob went down, rolling to his side, and when he looked up at Cable his eyes showed stunned surprise.

"You won't say anything like that again," Cable said.

22

Dancey had not taken his eyes off Cable. "You didn't give him a chance. Hitting him with a gun in your hand."

Cable glanced at him. "You're in a poor position to argue it."

"In fact," Dancey said, "you didn't give me much of a chance either. Now if you want to put the gun away and go about it fair—"

"That would be something, wouldn't it?"

Dancey said, "You're not proving anything with that gun in your hand."

"I don't have anything to prove."

"All right, then we leave for a while." Dancey looked over at Royce. "Get the stuff out of the house."

"Not now." Cable's voice stopped Royce. "You had a chance. You didn't take it. Now you leave without anything," Cable said. "Don't come back for it either. What doesn't burn goes in the river."

Royce said, "You think we won't be back?"

Cable's gaze shifted. "You'll ride into a double load of buckshot if you do. You can tell Kidston the same."

Royce seemed to grin. "Man, you're made to order. Duane's going to have some fun with you."

Dancey's eyes held on Cable. "So one man's going to stand us off."

"That's all it's taken so far."

"You think Vern's going to put up with you?"

"I don't see he has a choice," Cable answered.

"Then you don't know him," Dancey said flatly.

Chapter Two

With daylight a wind came out of the valley and he could hear it in the pines above the house.

Cable lay on his back listening, staring at the ceiling rafters. There was no sound in the room. Next to him, Martha was asleep. In the crib, beyond Martha's side of the bed, Sandy slept with his thumb and the corner of the blanket in his mouth. Clare and Davis were in the next room, in the log section of the house, and it was still too early even for them.

Later they would follow him around offering to help. He would be patient and let them think they were helping and answer all of their questions. He would think about the two and a half years away from them and he would kiss them frequently and study them, holding their small faces gently in his hands.

The wind rose and with it came the distant, dry-creaking sound of the barn door.

Later on he would see about the barn. Perhaps in the afternoon, if they had not come by then. This morning he would run Kidston's horses out of the meadow. Then perhaps Martha would have something for him to do.

They had worked until long after dark, sweeping, scrubbing, moving in their belongings. There would always be something more to be done; but that was all right because it was their home, something they had built themselves.

Just make sure everything that belonged to Royce and Joe Bob and Bill Dancey was out of here. Make dou-

24

ble sure of that. Then wait. No matter what he did, he would be waiting and listening for the sound of horses.

But there was nothing he could do about that. Don't worry about anything you can't do something about. When it's like that it just happens. It's like an act of God. Though don't blame God for sending Vern Kidston. Blame Vern himself for coming. If you can hate him it will be easier to fight him.

And there's always someone to fight, isn't there?

Ten years ago he had come here from Sudan, Texas—a nineteen-year-old boy seeking his future, working at the time for a freight company that hauled between Hidalgo and Tucson—and one night when they stopped at Denaman's Store he talked to John Denaman.

They sat on the loading platform with their legs hanging over the side, drinking coffee and now and then whisky, drinking both from the same cups, looking north into the vast darkness of the valley. John Denaman told him about the river and the good meadow land and the timber—ponderosa pine and aspen and willows, working timber and pretty-to-look-at timber. A man starting here young and working hard would have himself something in no time at all, Denaman had said.

But a man had to have money to buy stock with, Cable said. Something to build with.

No, Denaman said, not necessarily. He told about his man Acaso who'd died the winter before, leaving his two kids, Manuel and Luz, here and leaving the few cattle Denaman owned scattered through the hills. You're welcome to gather and work the cattle, Denaman said. Not more than a hundred head; but something to build on and you won't have to put up money till you market them and take your share.

That was something to think about, and all the way to Tucson Cable had pictured himself a rancher, a man with his own land, with his own stock. He thought, too, about a girl who lived in Sudan, Texas.

The first thing he did in Tucson was quit his job. The same day he bought twenty head of yearling stock, spending every last dollar he had, and drove his cattle the hundred and twenty miles back to the Saber River.

In the summer of his second year he built his own

adobe, with the help of Manuel Acaso, four miles north of the store. He sold some of his full-grown beef to the army at Fort Buchanan and he continued to buy yearlings, buying them cheap from people around Tubac who'd had enough of the Apache and were willing to make a small profit or none at all just to get shed of their stock and get out of southern Arizona.

The next year he left Manuel Acaso with his herd and traveled back to Sudan. The girl, Martha Sanford, was waiting for him. They were married within the week and he brought her home to the Saber without stopping for a honeymoon. Then he worked harder than he ever imagined a man could work and he remembered thinking during those days: nothing can budge you from this place. You are taking all there is to take and if you don't die you will make a success of it.

He was sure of it after living through the winter the Apaches came. They were Chiricahuas down out of the Dragoons and every few weeks they would raid his herd for meat. From November through April Cable lost over fifty head of cattle. But he made the Chiricahuas pay.

Lying prone high on the slope with a Sharps rifle, in the cover of the trees, he knocked two of them from their horses as they cut into his herd. The others came for him, squirming unseen through the pines, and when they rushed him he killed a third one with his revolver before they ran.

Another time that winter a war party attacked the house of Juan Toyopa, Cable's nearest neighbor to the west, killing Juan and his family and burning the house. They reached Cable's place at dawn—coming suddenly, screaming out of the grayness and battering against the door. He stood waiting with a revolver in each hand. Martha stood behind him with the shotgun. And when the door gave way he fired six rounds into them in half as many seconds. Two of the Apaches fell and Martha stepped over them to fire both shotgun loads at the Apaches running for the willows. One of them went down.

Then Cable rode to Denaman's to get Manuel Acaso. They returned to the willows, found the sign of six Chiricahuas and followed it all day, up into high desert country; and at dusk, deep in a high-walled canyon, they crept up to the dry camp of the six Apaches and shot three of

26

them before they could reach their horses. The survivors fled, at least one of them wounded, Cable was sure of that, and they never bothered him again.

Perhaps they believed his life was charmed, that he was beyond killing, and for that reason they stopped trying to take him or his cattle. And perhaps it was charmed, Cable had thought. Or else his prayers were being answered. It was a good thing to believe; it made him feel stronger and made him work even harder. That was the time he first had the thought: nothing can budge you from this land. Nothing.

The next year their first child was born. Clare. And Manuel Acaso helped him build the log addition to the house. He remembered planning it, lying here in this bed with Martha next to him and Clare, a month-old baby, in the same crib Sandy was sleeping in now; lying awake staring at the ceiling and thinking how he would build a barn after they'd completed the log room.

And now thinking about that time and not thinking about the years in between, he felt comfortable and at peace. Until the murmur of Martha's voice, close to him, brought him fully awake.

"They'll come today, won't they?"

He turned to her. She was on her side, her eyes open and watching him. "I guess they will."

"Is that what you were thinking about?"

Cable smiled. "I was thinking about the barn."

"You're not even worried, are you?"

"It doesn't do any good to show it."

"I thought you might be trying out your principle of not worrying about anything you can't do something about."

"Well, I thought about it."

Martha smiled. "Cabe, I love you."

He rolled to his side, pulling her close to him and kissed her, brushing her cheek and her mouth. His face remained close to hers. "We'll come out of this."

"We have to," Martha whispered.

When Cable left the house the sun was barely above the line of trees at the river's edge. The willow branches moved in the breeze, swaying slowly against the pale

27

morning sky. But soon, Cable knew, there would be sun glare and deep shadows, black against yellow, and the soft movement of the trees would be remembered from another time with another feeling.

With Davis and Clare he brought the four team horses out of the barn and put them on a picket line to graze. It wouldn't help to get them mixed with Kidston's herd. He saddled the sorrel gelding, but let the reins hang free so it could also graze. The sorrel wouldn't wander. After that he returned to the house.

Martha came out of the log room with Sandy. "What did you forget?"

"The Spencer," Cable said. He picked it up, then turned sharply, hearing Clare's voice.

The little girl ran in from the yard. "Somebody's coming!"

Cable stepped to the doorway. Behind him Martha called, "Davis— Clare, where is he?"

"He's all right." Cable lowered the Spencer looking out past Davis who was in the yard watching the rider just emerging from the trees. "It's Janroe."

The first thing Cable noticed about Janroe was that he wore two revolvers—one in a shoulder holster, the other on his hip—in addition to a shotgun in his saddle boot.

Then, as Janroe approached, he noticed the man's gaze. Taking it all in, Cable thought, seeing Janroe's eyes moving from the saddled gelding to the gear—cooking utensils, clothing, curl-toed boots, bedding and the three holstered revolvers on top—that was in a pile over by the barn.

Janroe reined in, his gaze returning to the adobe. "Well, you ran them, didn't you?" His hand touched his hat brim and he nodded to Martha, then fell away as Cable walked out to him. He made no move to dismount.

"I don't think you expected to see us," Cable said.

"I wasn't sure."

"But you were curious."

Janroe's gaze went to the pile of gear. "You took their guns," he said thoughtfully. "I'd like to have seen that." His eyes returned to Cable. "Yes, I would have given something to see that. Was anybody hurt?"

Cable shook his head.

"No shooting?"

"Not a shot."

"What'll you do with their stuff?"

"Leave it. They'll come back."

"I think I'd burn it."

"I thought about that," Cable said. "But I don't guess it's a way to make friends."

"You don't owe them anything."

"No, but I have to live with them."

Janroe glanced at the saddled horse. "You're going somewhere?"

"Out to the meadow."

"I'll ride along," Janroe said.

They passed into the willows, jumping their horses down the five-foot bank, and crossed a sandy flat before entering the brown water of the river. At midstream the water swirled chest high on the horses, then receded gradually until they again came up onto a stretch of sand before mounting the bank.

"Now you're going to run his horses?" Janroe asked.

"I'll move them around the meadow," Cable said. "Toward his land."

"He'll move them right back."

"We'll see."

"You've got a fight on your hands. You know that, don't you?"

They were moving out into the meadow toward Kidston's horse herd, walking their horses side by side, but now Cable reined to a halt.

"Look, I haven't even met Vern or Duane Kidston. First I'll talk to them. Then we'll see what happens."

Janroe shook his head. "They'll try to run you. If you don't budge, they'll shoot you out."

Cable said, "Are you going back now?"

Janroe looked at him with surprise. "I have time."

"And I've got work to do."

"Well," Janroe said easily, "I was going to try to talk you into going back to the store with me. I've got a proposition you ought to be interested in."

"Go ahead and make it."

"I've got to show you something along with it, and that's at the store."

"Then it'll have to wait," Cable said.

"Well"—Janroe shrugged—"it's up to you. I'll tell you this much, it would end your problem all at once."

Cable watched him closely. "What would I have to do?"

"Kill Vern," Janroe said mildly. "Kill him and his brother."

Cable had felt himself tensed, but now he relaxed. "Just like that."

"You can do it. You proved that the way you handled those three yesterday."

"And why are you so anxious to see the Kidstons dead?"

"I'm looking at it from your side."

"Like hell."

"All right." Janroe paused. "You were pretty close to John Denaman, weren't you?"

"He gave me my start here."

"Did you know Denaman was running guns for the South?"

Cable was watching Janroe closely. "You're sure?"

"He was just part of it," Janroe continued. "They're Enfield rifles shipped into Mexico by the British. Confederate agents bring them up over the border and the store is one of the relay points. It was Denaman's job to hide the rifles until another group picked them up for shipment east."

"And where do you come in?"

"When Denaman died I was sent out to take his place."

Cable's eyes remained on Janroe. So the man was a Confederate agent. And John Denaman had been one. That was hard to picture, because you didn't think of the war reaching out this far. But it was here. Fifteen hundred miles from the fighting, almost another world, but it was here.

"I told you," Janroe said, "I was with Kirby Smith. I lost my arm fighting the Yankees. When they said I wasn't any more use as a soldier I worked my way into this kind of a job. Eight months ago they sent me out here to take Denaman's place."

"And Manuel," Cable said. "Is he in it?"

Janroe nodded. "He scouts for the party that brings up the rifles. That's where he is now."

"When's he due back?"

"What do you want to do, check my story?"

"I was thinking of Manuel. I haven't seen him in a long time."

"He'll be back in a day or so."

"Does Luz know about the guns?"

"You can't live in the same house and not know about them."

"So that's what's bothering her."

Janroe looked at him curiously. "She said something to your wife?"

Cable shrugged off the question. "It doesn't matter. You started out with me killing Vern and Duane Kidston."

Janroe nodded. "How does it look to you now?"

"You're telling me to go after them. To shoot them down like you would an animal."

"Exactly."

"That's called murder."

"It's also called war."

Cable shook his head. "As far as I'm concerned the war's over."

Janroe watched him closely. "You don't stop believing in a cause just because you've stopped fighting."

"I've got problems of my own now."

"But what if there's a relation between the two? Between your problems and the war?"

"I don't see it."

"Open your eyes," Janroe said. "Vern supplies remounts to the Union army. He's doing as much to help them as any Yankee soldier in the line. Duane's organized a twelve-man militia. That doesn't sound like anything; but what if he found out about the guns? Good rifles that Confederate soldiers are waiting for, crying for. But even without that danger, once you see Duane you'll *want* to kill him. I'll testify before God to that."

Janroe leaned closer to Cable. "This is what I'm getting at. Shooting those two would be like aiming your rifle at Yankee soldiers. The only difference is you know their names."

Cable shook his head. "I'm not a soldier any more. That's the difference."

"You have to have a uniform on to kill?"

"You know what I mean."

"I know exactly what you mean," Janroe said. "You need an excuse. You need something to block off your conscience while you're pulling the trigger. Something like a license, so killing them won't be called murder."

Cable said nothing. He was listening, but staring off at the horse herd now.

Janroe watched him. "That's your problem. You want Vern and Duane off your land, but you don't have the license to hunt them. You don't have an excuse your conscience will accept." Janroe paused. He waited until Cable's gaze returned and he was looking directly into his eyes.

"I can give you that excuse, Mr. Cable. I can fix you up with the damnedest hunting license you ever saw, and your conscience will just sit back and laugh."

For a moment Cable was silent, letting Janroe's words run through his mind. All at once it was clear and he knew what the man was driving at. "If I worked for you," Cable said, "if I was an agent, I could kill them as part of my duty."

Janroe seemed to smile. "I could even order you to do it."

"Why me? If it's so important to you, why haven't you tried?"

"Because I can't afford to fool with something like that. If I'm caught, what happens to the gun running?"

"And if I fail," Cable said, "what happens to my family?"

"You don't have anything to lose," Janroe said easily. "What happens to them if Vern kills you? What happens to all of you if he runs you off your land?"

Cable shook his head. "I've never even seen these people and you want me to kill them."

"It will come to that," Janroe said confidently. "I'm giving you an opportunity to hit first."

"I appreciate that," Cable said. "But from now on, how would you like to keep out of my business? You stop worrying about me and I won't say anything about you. How will that be?" He saw the relaxed confidence drain from Janroe's face leaving an expressionless mask and a tight line beneath his mustache.

"I think you're a fool," Janroe said quietly. "But you won't realize it yourself until it's too late."

"All right," Cable said. He spoke calmly, not raising his voice, but he was impatient now, anxious for Janroe to leave. "That's about all I've got time for right now. You come out again some time, how's that?"

"If you're still around." Janroe flicked his reins and moved off.

Let him go, Cable thought, watching Janroe taking his time, just beginning to canter. He's waiting for you to call him. But he'll have a long wait, because you can do without Mr. Janroe. There was something about the man that was wrong. Cable could believe that Janroe had been a soldier and was now a Confederate agent; but his wanting the Kidstons killed—as if he would enjoy seeing it happen—that was something else. There was the feeling he wanted to kill them just for the sake of killing them, not for the reasons he brought up at all. Maybe it would be best to keep out of Janroe's way. There was enough to think about as it was.

Cable swung the sorrel in a wide circle across the meadow and came at the horse herd up wind, counting thirty-six, all mares and foals; seeing their heads rise as they heard him and caught his scent. And now they were moving, carefully at first, only to keep out of his way, then at a run as he spurred the sorrel toward them. Some tried to double back around him, but the sorrel answered his rein and swerved right and left to keep them bunched and moving.

Where the Saber crossed the valley, curving over to the east side of the meadow, he splashed the herd across with little trouble, then closed on them again and ran them as fast as the foals could move, up the narrowing, left-curving corridor of the valley. After what he judged to be four or five miles farther on, he came in sight of grazing cattle and there Cable swung away from the horse herd. This would be Kidston land.

Now he did not follow the valley back but angled for the near slope, crossed the open sweep of it to a gully which climbed up through shadowed caverns of ponderosa pine. At the crest of the hill he looked west out over tangled rock and brush country and beyond it to a towering near horizon of creviced, coldly silent stone. Close beyond this barrier was the Toyopa place, where Kidston now lived.

Cable followed the crest of the hill for almost a mile before he found a trail that descended the east slope. He moved along the narrowness of it, feeling the gradual slant beneath the sorrel, and seeing the valley again, down through open swatches in the trees. Soon he would be almost above the house. A few yards farther on he stopped.

Ahead of him, a young woman stood at the edge of the path looking down through the trees. Luz Acaso, Cable thought. No.

Luz came to his mind with the first glimpse of this girl in white. But Luz vanished as he saw blond hair—hair that was tied back with a ribbon and swirled suddenly over her shoulder as she turned and saw him.

This movement was abrupt, but now she stood watching him calmly. Her hand closed around the riding quirt suspended from her wrist and she raised it to hold it in front of her with both hands, not defensively, but as if striking a pose.

"I expected you to be older," the girl said. She studied him calmly, as if trying to guess his age or what he was thinking or what had brought him to this ridge.

Cable swung down from the saddle, his eyes on the girl. She was at ease—he could see that—and was still watching him attentively: a strikingly handsome girl, tall, though not as tall as Martha, and younger by at least six years, Cable judged.

He said, "You know who I am?"

"Bill Dancey told us about you." She smiled then. "With help from Royce and Joe Bob."

"Then you're a Kidston," Cable said.

"You'll go far," the girl said easily.

Cable frowned. "You're Vern's—daughter?"

"Duane's. I'm Lorraine, if that means anything to you."

"I don't know why," Cable said, "but I didn't picture your dad married."

Her eyebrows rose with sudden interest. "How did you picture him?"

"I don't know. Just average appearing."

Lorraine smiled. "You'll find him average, all right."

Cable stared at her. "You don't seem to hold much respect for him."

"I have no reason to."

"Isn't just because he's your father reason enough?"

Lorraine's all-knowing smile returned. "I knew you were going to say that."

"You did, huh? . . . How old are you?"

"Almost nineteen."

Cable nodded. That would explain some of it. "And you've been to school. You're above average pretty, which you'll probably swear to. And you've probably had your own way as long as you can remember."

"And if all that's true," Lorraine said. "Then what?"

Cable shook his head. "I don't know."

"What point are you trying to make?"

Cable smiled now. "You didn't react the way I thought you would."

"At least you're honest about it," Lorraine said. "Most men would have tried to bluster their way out. Usually they say, 'Well'—with what passes for a wise chuckle— 'you'll see things differently when you're a bit older.'" Lorraine's eyebrows rose. "Unfortunately, there isn't the least shred of evidence that wisdom necessarily comes with age."

"Uh-huh," Cable nodded. This girl could probably talk circles around him if he let her. But if she pulled that on Martha—

Cable smiled. "Why don't you come down and meet my wife?"

Lorraine hesitated. "I don't think I should put myself in the way."

"You wouldn't be in Martha's way. She'd be glad of the chance to sit down and talk."

"I wasn't referring to your wife. I meant my father.

He's coming, you know." She saw Cable's expression change. "Didn't you think he would?"

"Coming now?"

"As soon as he gathers his company," Lorraine answered. "Not Vern. Vern went up to Fort Buchanan yesterday on horse business." She looked away from Cable. "You know you can see your house right down there through the trees. I came here to watch."

She stepped back quickly as Cable moved past her, already urging his sorrel down the path as he mounted. She called out to him to wait, but he kept going and did not look back. Soon he was out of sight, following the long, gradual switchbacks that descended through the pines.

Martha had cleaned the stove for the second time. She came out of the house carrying a pail and at the end of the ramada she lifted it and threw the dirty water out into the sunlight. She watched it flatten and hang glistening gray before splattering against the hard-packed ground. She turned back to the house, hearing the sound of the horse then.

"Clare!" Her gaze flashed to the children playing in the aspen shade. They looked up and she called, not as loud, "Clare, bring the boys in for a while."

"Why do we have to—" Davis's voice trailed off. He made no move to rise from his hands and knees.

Martha looked back at the stable shed, then to the children. "Dave, I'm not going to call again." The children rose and came out of the trees.

She heard the horse again and with it a rustling, twig-snapping sound. She waved the children toward the house; but Clare hesitated, looking up toward the pines. "What's that noise?"

"Probably not anything," Martha said. "Inside now."

As they filed in, Cable turned the corner of the house. Martha let her breath out slowly and stood watching him as he dismounted and came toward her.

She wanted to say: Cabe, it's not worth it. One alarm after another, running the children inside every time there's a sound! But she looked at Cable's face and the words vanished.

"What is it?"

"They're on the way."

Martha glanced at the house, at the three children standing in the ramada shade watching them. "Clare, fix the boys a biscuit and jelly."

As she turned back, she again heard the rustling, muffled horse sound. She saw her husband's hand go to the Walker Colt a moment before Lorraine Kidston rounded the adobe.

"I decided," Lorraine said as she approached, "it would be more fun to watch from right here." She dropped her reins then, extending her arms to Cable. When he hesitated, she said, "Aren't you going to help me?"

Cable lifted her down from the side saddle, feeling her press against him, and he stepped back the moment her feet touched the ground. "Martha, this is Lorraine Kidston. Duane's girl."

Martha recognized his uneasiness. He wanted to appear calm, she knew, but he was thinking of other things. And she was aware of Lorraine's confidence. Lorraine was enjoying this, whatever it was, and for some reason she had Cable at a disadvantage. Martha nodded to Lorraine, listened as Cable explained their meeting on the ridge, and she couldn't help thinking: Soon we could be thrown to the lions and Lorraine has dressed in clean white linen to come watch.

"Come inside," Martha said pleasantly. "We can give you a chair at the window if you'd like."

Lorraine hesitated, but only for a moment. She nodded to Martha and said easily, "You're very kind."

At the door, the children stood staring at Lorraine. Martha named them as they entered the ramada shade, and reaching them, brushed Sandy's hair from his forehead. "The little Cables are about to have biscuits and jelly. Will you join them?"

"No, thank you," Lorraine said. She nodded politely to the children, but showed no interest in them, edging through the doorway now as if not wanting to touch them. Martha followed, moving the children to the table and sitting them down. Cable came in a moment later carrying the Spencer.

As he propped it against the wall between the two front windows, Lorraine said pleasantly, "I hope you're not going to shoot my father."

Cable closed both shutters of the right window, but only one shutter of the window nearer to the door. He turned then. "I hope not either."

"Oh, don't be so solemn," Lorraine said lightly. "If Duane does the talking you can be pretty sure he'll mess it up."

Cable saw Martha's momentary look of surprise. She placed a pan of biscuits on the table, watching Lorraine. "Miss Kidston," Cable said mildly, "doesn't have a very high regard for her father."

Martha straightened, wiping her hands on her apron. "That's nice."

Lorraine regarded her suspiciously. Then, as if feeling a compulsion to defend herself, she said, "If there is nothing about him personally to deserve respect, I don't see why it's due him just because he's a parent."

Cable was leaving it up to Martha now. He watched her, expecting her to reply, but Martha said nothing. The silence lengthened, weakening Lorraine's statement, demanding more from her.

"I don't suppose you can understand that," Lorraine said defensively.

"Hardly," Martha said, "since I've never met your father."

"You've met him," Lorraine said, glancing at Cable. "He's the kind who can say nothing but the obvious." Cable was looking out the window, paying no attention to her, and her gaze returned quickly to Martha.

"I know exactly what he's going to answer to every single thing I say," Lorraine went on. "One time it's empty wisdom, the next time wit. Now Vern, he's the other extreme. Vern sits like a grizzled stone, and at first you think it's pure patience. Then, after a few sessions of this, you realize Vern simply hasn't anything to say. I haven't yet decided which is worse, listening to Duane, or not listening to Vern."

"It sounds," Martha prompted, "as if you haven't been with them very long."

That brought it out. Lorraine recited a relaxed account of her life, using a tone bordering on indifference, though Martha knew Lorraine was enjoying it.

Her mother and father had separated when Lorraine was seven, and she had gone with her mother. That didn't mean it had taken her mother seven or eight years to learn what a monumental bore Duane was. She had simply sacrificed her best years on the small chance he might change. But finally, beyond the point of endurance, she left him, and left Gallipolis too, because that Ohio town seemed so typical of Duane. Wonderful years followed, almost ten of them. Then her mother died unexpectedly and she was forced to go to her father who was then in Washington. In the army. That was two or three years ago and she remained in Washington while Duane was off campaigning. Then he was relieved of his duty—though Duane claimed he "resigned his active commission"—and, unfortunately, she agreed to come out here with him. Now, after over a year with Duane and Vern, Lorraine was convinced that neither had ever had an original thought in his life.

Cable listened, his gaze going out across the yard and through the trees to the meadow beyond. You could believe only so much of that about Vern and Duane. Even if they were dull, boring old men to an eighteen-year-old girl, they could still run you or burn your house down or kill you or whatever the hell else they wanted. So don't misjudge them, Cable thought.

He heard Martha ask where they had lived and Lorraine answered Boston, New York City. Philadelphia for one season. They had found it more fun to move about.

Even with that tone, Martha will feel sorry for her, Cable thought, watching the stillness of the yard and the line of trees with their full branches hanging motionless over empty shade.

He tried to visualize the girl's mother and he pictured them—Lorraine and her mother—in a well-furnished drawing room filled with people. The girl moved from one group to another, nodding with her head tilted to one side, smiling now, saying something; then everyone in the group returning her smile at the same time.

Cable saw himself in the room—not intending it—but suddenly there he was; and he thought: That would be all right about now. Even though you wouldn't have anything to say and you'd just stand there—

He saw the first rider when he was midway across the river, moving steadily, V-ing the water toward the near bank. Now there were three more in the water and—Cable waited to make sure—two still on the other side. They came down off the meadow; and beyond them now, over their heads, Cable saw the grazing horse herd. They had returned the mares and foals.

As each man crossed the river, he dismounted quickly, handed off his horse and ran hunch-shouldered to the protection of the five-foot cutbank. One man was serving as horse holder, taking them farther down the bank where the trees grew more thickly.

Out of the line of fire, Cable thought. Behind him he heard Lorraine's voice. Then Martha's. But he wasn't listening to them now. This could be nine months ago, he thought, watching the trees and the river and the open meadow beyond. That could be Tishomingo Creek if you were looking down across a cornfield, and beyond it, a half mile beyond through the trees and briars, would be Bryce's Crossroads. But you're not standing in a group of eighty-five men now.

No, a hundred and thirty-five then, he thought. Forrest had Gatrel's Georgia Company serving with the escort.

How many of them would you like?

About four. That's all. Shotguns and pistols and the Kidstons wouldn't know what hit them. But now you're out-Forresting Forrest. He had two to one against him at Bryce's. And won. You've got six to one.

He could just see their heads now above the bank, spaced a few feet apart. He was still aware of Lorraine's voice, thinking now as he watched them: What are they waiting for?

A rifle barrel rose above the bank, pointed almost straight up, went off with a whining report and Lorraine stopped talking.

Cable turned from the window. "Martha, take the children into the other room." They watched him; the children, Martha, and Lorraine all watched him expectantly, but he turned back to the window.

He heard Lorraine say, "He's going to die when he finds out I'm here."

"He already knows," Cable said, not turning. "Your horse is outside."

Her voice brightened. "That's right!" She moved to Cable's side. "Now he won't know what to do."

"He's doing something," Cable said.

The rifle came up again, now with a white cloth tied to the end of the barrel, and began waving slowly back and forth.

"Surrender," Lorraine said mockingly, "or Major Kidston will storm the redoubts. This is too much."

Cable asked, "Is that him?"

Lorraine looked past his shoulder. Four men had climbed the bank and now came out of the trees, one a few paces ahead. He motioned the others to stop, then came on until he'd reached the middle of the yard. This one, the one Cable asked about, wore a beard, a Kossuth army hat adorned with a yellow, double-looped cord, and a brass eagle that pinned the right side of the brim to the crown; he wore cavalry boots and a flap-top holster on his left side, butt to the front and unfastened.

He glanced back at the three men standing just out from the trees, saw they had not advanced, then turned his attention again to the house, planting his boots wide and fisting his hands on his hips.

"Sometimes," Lorraine said, "Duane leaves me speechless."

"The first one's your father?" asked Cable, making sure.

"My God, who else?"

"That's Royce with the flag," Cable said.

"And Joe Bob and Bill Dancey in reserve," Lorraine said. "I think Bill looks uncomfortable."

Cable's eyes remained on her father. "Where's Vern?"

"I told you, he went to Fort Buchanan," Lorraine answered. Her attention returned to her father. "He loves to pose. I think right now he's being Sheridan before Missionary Ridge. Wasn't it Sheridan?"

"Cable!"

"Now he speaks," Lorraine said gravely, mockingly.

"Cable—show yourself!"

Cable moved past Lorraine into the open doorway. He looked out at Duane. "I'm right here."

Duane's fist came off his hips. For a moment before he spoke, his eyes measured Cable sternly. "Where do you have my daughter?"

"She's here," Cable said.

Again Duane stared in silence, his eyes narrowed and his jaw set firmly. The look is for your benefit, Cable thought. He's not concentrating as much as he's acting. He saw Duane then take a watch from his vest pocket, thumb it open and glance at the face.

Duane looked up. "You have three minutes by the clock to release my daughter. If you don't, I will not be responsible for what happens to you."

"I'm not holding her."

"You have three minutes, Mr. Cable."

"Listen, she came on her own. She can walk out any time she wants." Behind him he heard Lorraine laugh.

Cable looked at her. "You'd better go out to him."

"No, not yet," she said. "Call his bluff and let's see what he does."

"Listen, while you're being entertained my wife and children are likely to get shot."

"He wouldn't shoot while I'm in here."

"That's something we're not going to find out." Cable's hand closed on her arm. Lorraine pulled back; but he held her firmly and drew her into the doorway. He saw Duane return the watch to his pocket, and saw a smile of confidence form under the man's neatly trimmed beard.

"All of a sudden, Mr. Cable, you seem a bit anxious," Duane said. His hands went to his hips again.

Close to him, as Cable urged her through the door, Lorraine gasped theatrically, "Would you believe it!"

"Go on now," Cable whispered. To Duane he said, "I told you once I wasn't holding your daughter. What do I have to do to convince you?"

Duane's expression tightened. "You keep quiet till I'm ready for you!" His gaze shifted to Lorraine who now stood under the ramada a few steps from Cable and half turned toward him. She stood patiently with her arms folded. "Lorraine, take your horse and go home."

"I'd rather stay." She glanced at Cable, winking at him.

"This is not something for you to see," Duane said gravely.

"I don't want to miss your big scene," Lorraine said. "I can feel it coming."

"Lorraine—I'm warning you!"

"Oh, stop it. You aren't warning anyone."

Duane's voice rose. "I'm not going to tell you again!"

Smiling, Lorraine shook her head. "If you could only see yourself."

"Lorraine—"

"All right." She stopped him, raising her hands. "I surrender." She laughed again, shaking her head, then moved unhurriedly to her horse, mounted and walked it slowly across the yard, smiling pleasantly at her father, her head turning to watch him until she was beyond his line of vision. She passed into the willow trees.

She's had her fun, Cable thought, watching her. But now the old man is mad and he'll take it out on you. Cable's gaze returned to Duane. You mean he'll try. At this moment he did not feel sorry for Duane; even after Duane had been made to look ridiculous by his own daughter. No, if Duane pushed him he would push him back. There was not time to laugh at this pompous little man with the General Grant beard; because beyond his theatrics this was still a matter of principle, of pride, of protecting his family, of protecting his land. A matter of staying alive too.

Cable said bluntly, "Now what?"

"Now," Duane answered, drawing his watch again, "you have until twelve o'clock noon to pack your belongings and get out." He looked down at the watch. "A little less than three hours."

There it is, Cable thought wearily. You expected it and there it is. He looked over his shoulder, glancing back at his wife, then turned back to Duane.

"Mr. Kidston, I'm going to talk to my wife first. You just hang on for a minute." He stepped back, swinging the door closed.

"Well?" he asked.

"This is yesterday," Martha said, "with the places reversed."

Cable smiled thinly. "We don't make friends very easy, do we?"

"I don't think it matters," Martha said quietly, "whether Mr. Kidston likes us or not."

"Then we're staying," Cable said.

"Did you think we wouldn't?"

"I wasn't sure."

Martha went to the bedroom. She looked in at the children before coming to Cable. "Clare's doing her letters for the boys."

"Martha, make them stay in there."

"I will."

"Then stand by the window with the shotgun, but don't shove the barrel out until I'm out there and they're looking at me."

"What will you do?"

"Talk to him. See how reasonable he is."

"Do you think Vern is there?"

"No. I guess Vern does the work while Duane plays war."

Martha's lips parted to speak, but she smiled then and said nothing.

"What were you going to say?" Cable asked.

She was still smiling, a faint smile that was for Cable, not for herself. "I was going to tell you to be careful, but it sounded too typical."

He smiled with her for a moment, then said, "Ready?" She nodded and Cable turned to the door. He opened it, closed it behind him, and stepped out to the shade of the ramada.

Duane Kidston had not moved; but Royce, holding the carbine with the white cloth, had come up on his right. Bill Dancey and Joe Bob remained fifteen to twenty feet behind them, though they had moved well apart.

"You have exactly"—Duane studied his watch—"two hours and forty-three minutes to pack and get out. Not a minute more."

Cable moved from shade to sunlight. He approached Duane, seeing him shift his feet and pocket his watch, and he heard Royce say, "Don't let him get too close."

Then Duane: "That's far enough!"

Cable ignored this. He came on until less than six feet separated him from Duane.

"I thought if we didn't have to shout," Cable said, "we could straighten this out."

"There's nothing to straighten," Duane said stiffly.

"Except you're trying to run me from my own land."

"That assumption is the cause of your trouble," Duane said. "This doesn't happen to be your land."

"It has been for ten years now."

"This property belonged to a Confederate sympathizer," Duane said. "I confiscated it in the name of the United States government, and until a court decides legal ownership, it remains ours."

"And if we don't leave?"

"I will not be responsible for what happens."

"That includes my family?"

"Man, this is a time of war! Often the innocent must suffer. But that is something I can do nothing to prevent."

"You make it pretty easy for yourself," Cable said.

"I'm making it easy for *you!*" Duane paused, as if to control the rage that had colored his face. "Listen, the easy way is for you to load your wagon and get out. I'm giving you this chance because you have a family. If you were alone, I'd take you to Fort Buchanan as a prisoner of war." Duane snapped his fingers. "Like that and without any talk."

"Even though I'm no longer a soldier?"

"You're still a Rebel. You fought for an enemy of the United States. You likely even killed some fine boys working for that bushwhacker of a Bedford Forrest and I'll tell you this, whether you're wearing a uniform or not, if it wasn't for your family, I'd do everything in my power to destroy you."

Joe Bob shifted his weight from one leg to the other. "That's tellin' him, Major." He winked, grinning at Bill Dancey.

Duane glanced over his shoulder, but now Joe Bob's face showed nothing. He stood lazily, with his hip cocked, and only nodded as Duane said, "I'll do the talking here."

Like yesterday, Cable thought. They're waiting to eat

you up. His gaze shifted from Royce and Duane to Joe Bob.

Just like yesterday—

And the time comes and you can't put it off.

Cable's gaze swung back to Duane, though Joe Bob was still in his vision, and abruptly he said, "There's a shotgun dead on you." He waited for the reaction, waited for Joe Bob's mind to snap awake and realize what he meant. And the moment the man's eyes shifted to the house, Cable acted. He drew the Walker Colt, thumbed back the hammer and leveled it at Duane's chest. It happened quickly, unexpectedly; and now there was nothing Duane or any of his men could do about it.

"Now get off my land," Cable said. "Call a retreat, Major, or *I* won't be responsible for what happens."

An expression of shocked surprise showed in Duane's eyes and his mouth came open even before he spoke. "We're here under a flag of truce!"

"Take your flag with you."

"You can't pull a gun during a truce!"

"It's against the rules?"

Duane controlled his voice. "It is a question of honor. Something far beyond your understanding."

Royce stood with the truce-flag carbine cradled over one arm, holding it as if he'd forgotten it was there. "He makes it worthwhile. You got to give him that."

"Major"—Joe Bob's voice—"are you a chance-taking man? I was thinking, if you were quick on your feet—"

"I told you to keep out of this!" Duane snapped the words at him.

Looking at Duane as he spoke, at him and past him, Cable saw the horse and rider coming up out of the river, crossing the sand flat, climbing the bank now.

"I was just asking," Joe Bob said lazily. "If you thought you could flatten quick enough, we'd cut him in two pieces."

The rider approached them now, walking his horse out of the willows. A moment before they heard the hoof sounds, Cable said, "Tell your man to stay where he is."

Joe Bob saw him first and called out, "Vern, you're missing it!" Royce and Dancey turned as Joe Bob spoke, but Duane's eyes held on Cable.

"You've waited too long," Duane said.

Cable backed off a half step, still holding the Walker on Duane; but now he watched Vern Kidston as he approached from beyond Dancey, passing him now, sitting heavily and slightly stooped in the saddle, his eyes on Cable as he came unhurriedly toward him. A few yards away he stopped but made no move to dismount.

With his hat forward and low over his eyes, the upper half of his face was in shadow, and a full mustache covering the corners of his mouth gave him a serious, solemn look. He was younger than Duane—perhaps in his late thirties—and had none of Duane's physical characteristics. Vern was considerably taller, but that was not apparent now. The contrast was in their bearing and Cable noticed it at once. Vern was Vern, without being conscious of himself. Thoughts could be in his mind, but he did not give them away. You were aware of only the man, an iron-willed man whose authority no one here questioned. In contrast, Duane could be anyone disguised as a man.

Vern Kidston sat with his hands crossed limply over the saddle horn. He sat relaxed, obviously at ease, staring down at this man with the Walker Colt. Then, unexpectedly, his eyes moved to Bill Dancey.

"You were supposed to meet me this morning. Coming back I stopped up on the summer meadow and waited two hours for you."

"Duane says come with him else I was through," Dancey said calmly, though a hint of anger showed in his bearded face. "Maybe we ought to clear this up, just who I take orders from."

Vern Kidston looked at his brother then. "I go up to Buchanan for one day and you start taking over."

"I'd say running this man off your land is considerably more important than selling a few horses," Duane said coldly.

"You would, uh?" Vern's gaze shifted. His eyes went to the house, then lowered. "So you're Cable."

Cable looked up at him. "I've been waiting for you."

"I guess you have."

"Vern"—it was Duane's voice—"he pulled his gun under a sign of truce!"

Kidston looked at his brother. "I'd say the issue is

47

he's still holding it." His eyes returned to Cable. "One man standing off four." He paused thoughtfully. "His Colt gun doesn't look that big to me."

Cable moved the Walker from Duane to Vern. "How does it look now?"

Vern seemed almost to smile. "There's seven miles of nerve between pointing a gun and pulling the trigger."

Cable stared at him, feeling his hope of reasoning with Kidston dissolve. But it was momentary. It was there with the thought: He's like the rest of them. His mind's made up and there's no arguing with him. Then the feeling was gone and the cold rage crept back into him, through him, and he told himself: But you don't budge. You know that, don't you? Not one inch of ground.

"Mr. Kidston," Cable said flatly, "I've fought for this land before. I've even had to kill for it. I'm not proud of saying that, but it's a fact. And if I have to, I'll kill for it again. Now if you don't think this land belongs to me, do something about it."

"I understand you have a family," Kidston said.

"I'll worry about my family."

"They wouldn't want to see you killed right before their eyes."

Cable cocked his wrist and the Walker was pointed directly at Vern's face. "It's your move, Mr. Kidston."

Vern sat relaxed, his hands still crossed on the saddle horn. "You know you wouldn't have one chance of coming out of this alive."

"How good are your chances?"

"Maybe you wouldn't have time to pull the trigger."

"If you think they can shoot me before I do, give the word."

Twenty feet to Cable's right, Joe Bob said, "Wait him out, Vern. He can't stand like that all day. Soon as his arm comes down I'll put one clean through him."

Dancey said, "And the second you move the shotgun cuts you in two."

Vern's eyes went to the house. "His wife?"

"Look close," Dancey said. "You see twin barrels peeking out the window. I'd say she could hold it resting on the ledge longer than we can stand here."

Vern studied the house for some moments before his

gaze returned to Cable. "You'd bring your wife into it? Risk her life for a piece of land?"

"My wife killed a Chiricahua Apache ten feet from where you're standing," Cable said bluntly. "They came like you've come and she killed to defend our home. Maybe you understand that. If you don't, I'll say only this. My wife will kill again if she has to, and so will I."

Thoughtfully, slowly, Kidston said, "Maybe you would." A silence followed until his eyes moved to Duane. "Go on home. Take your cavalry and get."

"I'm going," Duane said coldly. "I'm going to Fort Buchanan. If you can't handle this man, the army can."

"Duane, you're going home."

"I have your word you'll attend to him?"

"Go on, get out of here."

Duane hesitated, as if thinking of a way to salvage his self-respect, then turned without a word and walked off.

Kidston looked at his three riders. None of them had moved. "Go with him. And take your gear."

They stood lingeringly until Vern's gaze returned to Cable. That dismissed them and they moved away, picked up the gear Cable had piled by the barn and followed Duane to the willows.

"Well," Cable said, "are we going to live together?"

"I don't think you'll last."

"Why?"

"Because," Kidston said quietly, "you're one man; because you've got a family; because your stomach's going to be tied in a knot wondering when I'm coming. You won't sleep. And every time there's a sound you'll jump out of your skin. . . . Your wife will tell you it isn't worth it; and after a while, after her nerves are worn raw, she'll stop speaking to you and acting like a wife to you, and you won't see a spark of life in her."

Cable's gaze went to the house and he called out, "Martha!" After a moment the door opened and Martha came out with the shotgun under her arm. Kidston watched her, removing his hat as she neared them and holding it in his hand. He stood with the sun shining in his face and on his hair that was dark and straight and pressed tightly to his skull with perspiration. He nodded as Cable introduced them and put on his hat again.

"Mr. Kidston says we'll leave because we won't be able to stand it," Cable said now. "He says the waiting and not knowing will wear our nerves raw and in the end we'll leave of our own accord."

"What did you say?" Martha asked.

"I didn't say anything."

"I don't suppose there's much you could." She looked off toward the willows, seeing the men there mounting and starting across the river, then looked at her husband again. "Well, Cabe," she said, "are you going to throw Mr. Kidston out or ask him in for coffee?"

"I don't know. What do you think?"

"Perhaps Mr. Kidston will come back," Martha answered, "when we're more settled."

"Perhaps I will," Kidston said. His eyes remained on Martha: a woman who could carry a shotgun gracefully and whose eyes were dark and clear, warmly clear, and who stared back at him calmly and with confidence. He recalled the way she had walked out to meet him, with the sun on her dark hair, coming tall and unhurried with the faint movement of her legs beneath the skirt.

"Maybe you'll stay at that," Vern said, still looking at Martha. "Maybe you're the kind that would."

Cable watched him walk off toward the willows, and he was trying to picture this solemn-faced man kissing Luz Acaso.

For the rest of the morning and through the afternoon, there was time to think about Kidston and wonder what he would do; but there was little time for Cable and Martha to talk about him.

Vern wanted the land and if Cable didn't move, if he couldn't be frightened off the place, he would be forced off at gun point. It was strange; Vern was straightforward and easy to talk to. You believed what he said and knew he wasn't scheming or trying to trick you. Still, he wanted the land; and if waiting wouldn't get it for him, he would take it. That was clear enough.

Cable chopped wood through the afternoon, stacking a good supply against the back wall of the adobe. Soon he'd be working cattle again and there would be little time for close to home chores.

Then, after supper, he heard the creaking barn door. If the wind rose in the night, the creaking sound would become worse and wake him up. He would lie in bed thinking and losing sleep. You could think too much about something like this; Cable knew that. You could picture too many possibilities of failure and in the end you could lose your nerve and run for it. Sometimes it was better to let things just happen, to be ready and try to do the right thing, but just not think about it so much.

So he went out into the dusk to see about the door. Carrying an unlit lantern, Cable opened the door and stepped into the dim stillness of the barn. He hung the lantern on a peg and was bringing his arms down when the gun barrel pushed into his back.

"Now we'll do it our way," Joe Bob said.

Chapter Three

Royce lifted the Walker from Cable's holster. He stepped back and Joe Bob came in swinging, hooking his right hand hard into Cable's cheek. In the semi-darkness there was a grunt and a sharp smacking sound and Cable was against the board wall. Joe Bob turned him, swinging again, and broke through Cable's guard. He waded in then, grunting, slashing at Cable's face with both fists, holding him pinned to the boards, now driving a mauling fist low into Cable's body, then crossing high with the other hand to Cable's face. Joe Bob worked methodically, his fists driving in one after the other, again and again and again, until Cable's legs buckled. He had not been able to return a blow or even cover himself and now his back eased slowly down the boards. Joe Bob waited, standing stoop-shouldered and with his hands hanging heavily. Then his elbows rose; he went back a half step, came in again and brought his knee up solidly into Cable's jaw.

Abruptly, Royce said, "Listen!"

There was no sound except for Joe Bob's heavy, open-mouthed breathing. The silence lengthened until Royce said, between a whisper and a normal tone, "I heard somebody."

"Where?"

"Shhh!" Royce eased toward the open door.

"Cabe?" It came from outside. Martha's voice.

Royce let his breath out slowly. He stepped into the doorway and saw Martha in the gray dusk. She was perhaps forty feet from him, near the corner of the house.

"Who is it?"

"Evening, Mrs. Cable."

"Who's there?"

"It's just me. Royce." He stepped outside.

"Where's my husband?"

"Inside. Me and Joe Bob came back for some stuff we left"—he was moving toward her now—"and your husband's helping us dig it out."

She called past Royce. "Cabe?"

No answer. Five seconds passed, no more than that, then Martha had turned and was running—around the corner of the log section to the dark shadow of the ramada, hearing him behind her as she pushed the door open into bright lamplight and swung it closed. She heard him slam against it, hesitated—*Hold the door or go for the shotgun!*—saw Clare wide-eyed and said, "Go to the other room!" Martha was near the stove, raising the shotgun when Royce burst into the room. His hand was under the barrel as she pulled the trigger and the blast exploded up into the ceiling.

Royce threw the shotgun aside. He stood breathing in and out heavily. "You like to killed me."

"Where's my husband?"

"Old Joe Bob's straightening things out with him."

She was aware of the children crying then. Past Royce, she saw them just inside the bedroom. Clare's face was red and glistened with tears. And because she cried, Sandy was crying, with his lower lip pouted and his eyes tightly closed. Davis was staring at Royce. His eyes were round and large and showed natural fear, but he stood with his fists balled and did not move.

"There's nothing to cry about," Martha said. "Come kiss me good night and go to bed." They stood in their flannel nightshirts, afraid now to come into the room. Martha started for them, but she stopped.

Cable stood in the doorway. Joe bob pushed him from behind and he lurched in, almost going to his knees, but caught himself against the back of a chair. Davis watched his father. His sister and brother were still crying, whimpering, catching their breath.

Abruptly both children stopped, their eyes on Joe Bob as he came toward them. He said nothing, and no more than glanced at them before slamming the bedroom door in their faces. Immediately their crying began again, though now the sound was muffled by the heavy door.

Martha poured water from the kettle, saturating a dish towel; she wrung the water from it and brought it to Cable who was bent over the back of the chair, leaning heavily on it with his arms supporting him stiffly.

"Cabe, are you all right?"

He took the towel from her, pressing it to his mouth, then looked at the blood on the cloth and folded it over, touching it to his mouth again. His teeth throbbed with a dullness that reached up into his head. He could not feel his lips move when he spoke.

"It's not as bad as it looks."

Joe Bob said, "Then maybe I should give you some more."

Martha turned the chair around, helping her husband sit down.

Cable's eyes raised. "The children—?"

"They're all right. They're frightened, that's all."

"You better go talk to them."

"You better not," Joe Bob said. "They'll shut up after a while."

Martha looked at him now. "What do you want?"

"I'm not sure," Joe Bob said. "We're taking one step at a time." He glanced at Royce. "I wish Austin and Wynn were here." He was referring to his two brothers who also worked for Kidston. "They'd have some ideas. Man, would they!"

"Do you want us to leave?" asked Martha.

"Not right yet." Joe Bob glanced at Royce again, winking this time. "We might think of something." His gaze went beyond Royce, moving over the room and coming back to Martha. "You're such a fine housekeeper, maybe we'll keep you here." He winked at Royce again. "How'd you like to keep house for us?"

Martha did not speak, but she held Joe Bob's gaze until he grinned and moved away from her, going toward the kitchen cupboards.

"I don't know if I'd want her," Royce said. "She like to took my head off."

"I heard," Joe Bob said. He had opened a top cupboard and was reaching up into it. "Man, look at this." He took down an almost-full whisky bottle, smiling now and looking at Cable as he turned. "Would you've thought it of him?" Joe Bob uncorked the bottle and took a drink. "Man—"

Royce was next to him now, taking the bottle and drinking from it. He scowled happily, wiping his hand across his mouth. "Now this puts a different light on the subject."

Joe Bob took the bottle again, extending it to Martha. "Sweetie?"

"No, thank you."

"Just a little one."

Royce said, "Don't pour it away. If she doesn't want any, all right." He watched Joe Bob lift the bottle and snatched it from him as it came down. Now he took his time, smiling, looking at the label before he drank again.

"I think we ought to sit down," Royce said. "Like at a party."

"And talk to her about staying," Joe Bob said.

Royce grinned. "Wouldn't that be something."

"Man, picture it."

"Maybe we'd even pay her."

"Sure we would. With love and affection."

Cable said, "Does Vern know you're here?"

Royce looked at Cable. "Maybe I ought to take a turn on him."

"Help yourself," Joe Bob said.

"Vern and I agreed to settle this ourselves," Cable said.

Joe Bob looked at Royce. "He don't talk so loud now, does he?"

"He knows better," Royce said.

Joe Bob nodded thoughtfully. He drank from the bottle before saying, "You think we need him?"

"What for?" Royce took the bottle.

"That's the way I feel."

"Hell, throw him out."

"What about the kids—throw them out too?"

"Do you hear any kids? They're asleep already. Kids forget things a minute later." Royce lifted the bottle.

"Just throw him out, uh?"

"Sure. He'll lay out there like a hound. Else he'll

crawl away. One way or the other, what difference does it make?"

Joe Bob considered this. "He can't go for help. Where'd he go, to Vern? To the one-arm man?"

Royce nodded. "Maybe to Janroe."

"So he does," Joe Bob said. "How's the one-arm man going to help him?" Joe Bob shook his head. "He's in a miserable way."

"Sure he is."

"Too miserable."

"Don't feel sorry for him."

"I mean, put him out of his misery."

Now Royce said nothing.

"Not us do it," Joe Bob said. "Him do it."

"I don't follow."

"You don't have to." Joe Bob drank from the bottle, then stood holding it, staring at Cable. "As long as he does." After a moment he handed Royce the bottle and walked over to Cable.

"You understand me, don't you?"

Cable straightened against the back of the chair. He shook his head.

"You will." Joe Bob stood close to him, looking down, and said then, "You're a miserable man, aren't you?"

Cable sat tensed. He could not fight Joe Bob now and there was nothing he could say. So he remained silent, his eyes going to Martha who stood with her hands knotted into slender fists. Still with his eyes on Martha, he felt the sudden, sharp pain in his scalp and in a moment he was looking up into Joe Bob's tight-jawed face.

Close to his belt, Joe Bob held Cable's head back, his hand fisted in Cable's hair. "I asked if you're a miserable man!"

Cable tried to swallow, but most of the blood-saliva remained in his mouth. He said, "I'd be a liar if I said I wasn't." The words came hesitantly, through swollen lips. But he stared up at Joe Bob calmly, breathing slowly, and only when he saw the man's expression change did he try to push up out of the chair. Then it was too late.

He went back with the chair as Joe Bob's fist slammed into his face. On the floor he rolled to his side, then raised himself slowly to his hands and knees. Joe Bob stood looking down at him with both fists balled and his jaw clenched in anger.

"I hate a man who thinks he's smart. God, I hate a man who does that."

Joe Bob was feeling the whisky. It showed in his face; and the cold, quiet edge was gone from the tone of his voice. On Royce, the whisky was having an opposite effect. He was grinning, watching Joe Bob with amusement; and now he said, "If he bothers you, throw him out. That's all you got to do."

"Better than that," Joe Bob said. He extended a hand to Royce though his eyes remained on Cable. "Give me his Colt."

"Sure." Royce pulled the revolver from his belt and put it in Joe Bob's hand. He stepped back, watching with interest as Joe Bob turned the cylinder to check the load.

"You're going to kill him?"

"You'll see." Joe Bob cocked the revolver. He pointed it at Cable and motioned to the door. "Walk outside."

Cable came to his feet. He looked at Martha, then away from her and walked toward the open door, seeing the dark square of it, then the deep shadow of the ramada as he neared the door, and beyond it, over the yard, a pale trace of early moonlight.

Now he was almost in the doorway, and the boot steps came quickly behind him. He was pushed violently through the opening, stumbled as he hit the ground and rolled out of the deep shadow of the ramada. He pushed himself to his knees, then fell flat again as Joe Bob began firing from the doorway. With the reports he heard Martha's scream. And as suddenly as the gunfire began, it was over. He heard Joe Bob say, "I wasn't aiming at him. If I was aiming he'd be dead. I got rid of four rounds is all."

Joe Bob leaned in the doorway looking out into the darkness, the whisky warm inside of him and feeling Royce and the woman watching him. He would make it good, all right. Something Royce would tell everybody about.

He called out to Cable, "One left, boy. Put yourself out of your misery and save Vern and me and everybody a lot of trouble. Pull the trigger and it's all over. Nobody worries any more."

He flipped the Walker in his hand, held it momentarily by the barrel, then threw it side-arm out to the yard. The revolver struck the ground, skidded past Cable, and the door slammed closed.

What would Forrest do?

That was a long time ago.

But what would he do? Cable thought.

He'd call on them to surrender. Not standing the way Duane stood, but with a confidence you could feel. The Yankees felt it and that part was real. He'd convince them he had more men and more artillery than they did—by having more buglers than companies and by having the same six field pieces come swinging down around the hill and into the woods, which was the reason the Yankee raider, Streight, surrendered—and only that part was unreal. And if they didn't surrender, he'd find their weak point and beat the living hell out of it.

But these two won't surrender. You're seven hundred miles away from that. So what's their weak point?

Almost a quarter of an hour had passed since the door slammed closed. Cable lay on his stomach, on the damp sand at the edge of the river. He bathed his face, working his jaw and feeling the soreness of it, and rinsed his mouth until the inside bleeding stopped. The Walker Colt, with one load in it, was in his holster. And now what?

Now you think it out and do it and maybe it will work. Whatever it is.

What would Forrest do?

Always back to him, because you know he'd do something. God, and Nathan Bedford Forrest, I need help. God's smile and Forrest's bag of tricks.

When too many things crowded into Cable's mind, he would stop thinking. He would calm himself, then tell himself to think very slowly and carefully. A little anger was good, but not rage; that hindered thinking. He tried not to think of Martha, because thinking of her and picturing her with them and wondering made it more difficult to take this coldly, to study it from all sides.

Two and a half years ago, he thought, you wouldn't be lying here. You'd be dead. You'd have done something foolish and you'd be dead. But you have to hurry. You still have to hurry.

But even thinking this, and not being able to keep the picture of them with Martha out of his mind, he kept himself calm.

He was thankful for having served with Forrest. You learned things watching Forrest and you learned things getting out of the situations Forrest got you into. There had been times like this—not the same because there was Martha and the children now—but there had been out-numbered times and one-bullet times and lying close to the ground in the moonlight times. And he had come through them.

Their weak point, Cable thought. Or their weakness.

Whisky . . . its effect on Joe Bob. His act of bra-vado, throwing the one-load revolver out after him, telling him to use it on himself.

What if he did?

What it they heard a shot and thought he did? Would they come outside? The one-load revolver could be Joe Bob's mistake. His weak point.

There it was. A possibility. Would one come out, or both? Or neither?

Just get them out, he thought. Stop thinking and get them out. He crawled on his hands and knees along the water's edge until he found a rock; one with smooth edges, heavy enough and almost twice the size of his fist. He rose now, moved back to the chest-high bank, climbed it and stood in the dark willow shadows. Drawing the revolver, cocking it, he moved closer to the trunk of the willow. Then, pointing the barrel directly at the ground, he squeezed the trigger.

The report was loud and close to him, then fading, fading and leaving a ringing that stretched quickly to silence; and now even the night sounds that had been in the trees and in the meadow across the river were gone.

Through the heavy-hanging branches he watched the house; picturing Joe Bob standing still in the room. Won-der about it, Cable thought. But not too long. Look at your friend who's looking at you and both of you wonder about it. Then decide. Come on, decide right now. Somebody has to come out and make sure. You don't believe it, but you'd like to believe it, so you have to come see. Decide that one of you has to watch Martha. So only one of you can come out. Come on, get it through your head! That's the way it has to be!

And finally the door opened.

He saw a man framed in the doorway with the light behind him. The man stood half turned, talking back into the room. Then he stepped outside, drawing his revolver. Another figure appeared in the doorway, but the man outside came on alone. Cable let his breath out slowly.

He stood close to the trunk of the tree now, holding the rock against his stomach, watching the man coming carefully across the yard. He was not coming directly toward Cable, but would enter the trees about twelve or fifteen feet from him.

Now he was nearing the trees, moving cautiously and listening. He came on and a moment later was in the willows, out of sight.

"I don't see him!" The voice came from the trees, shouted toward the house. It was Royce.

From the doorway, Joe Bob called back, "Look along the bank."

Cable waited. He heard Royce. Then saw him, moving along the bank, stepping carefully and looking down at the sand flat. Cable tightened against the tree, waiting. Now Royce was near, now ducking under the branches of Cable's tree—his revolver in his right hand, on the side away from Cable. Royce stepped past him and stopped.

"I don't see him!"

From the house: "Keep looking!"

Royce started off, looking down at the sand flat again. Cable was on him in two strides, bringing the rock back as he came, holding on to it and slamming it against the side of Royce's head as the man started to turn. Cable's momentum carried both of them over the bank. He landed on Royce with his hand on the revolver barrel and came up holding it, cocking it, not bothering with Royce now, but ducking down as he wheeled to climb out of the cutbank and into the trees again.

From the house: "Royce?"

Silence.

"Royce, what'd you do?"

Take him, Cable thought. Before he goes back inside. Before he has time to think about it.

He took the barrel of the revolver in his left hand. He wiped his right hand across the front of his shirt, stretched his fingers, opening and closing his hand, then gripped the revolver again and moved out of the trees.

Joe Bob saw him and called out, "Royce?"

Cable remembered thinking one thing: You should have taken Royce's hat. But now it was too late. He was in the open moving across the yard that was gray and shadow-streaked with moonlight.

"Royce, what's the matter with you!"

Cable was perhaps halfway across the yard when he stopped. He half turned, planting his feet and bringing up the revolver; he extended it straight out, even with his eyes, and said, "Joe Bob—" Only that.

And for a moment the man stood still. He knew it was Cable and the knowing it held him in the light-framed doorway unable to move. But he had to move. He had to fall back into the room or go out or draw. And it had to be done *now*—

Cable was ready. He saw Joe Bob's right-hand revolver come out, saw him lunging for the darkness of the ramada and he squeezed the trigger on this suddenly moving target. Without hesitating he lowered the barrel, aiming at where Joe Bob would have to be and fired again; then a third time; and when the heavy, ringing sound died away there was only silence.

He walked through the fine smoke to where Joe Bob lay, face-down with his arms outstretched in front of him. Standing over him, he looked up to see Martha in the doorway.

"It's all right now," Cable said. "It's all over."

"Is he dead?"

Cable nodded.

And Royce was dead.

Now, remembering the way he had used the rock, swinging viciously because there was one chance and only one, Cable could see how it could have killed Royce. But he hadn't *intended* killing Joe Bob. He had wanted badly to hold a gun on him and fire it and see him go down, doing it thoroughly because with Joe Bob also he would have only one momentary chance; but that was not the same as wanting to kill.

Cable found their horses in the pines above the barn. He led them down to the yard and slung the two men face-down over the saddles, tying them on securely. After that he took the horses across the river and let them go to find their way home. Let Vern see them now, if he put them up to it. Even if he didn't, let him bury them; they were his men.

When Cable returned to the house he said, "In the morning we'll go see Janroe. We'll ask him if you and the children can board at the store."

Martha watched him. "And you?"

"I'll come back here."

Bill Dancey came in while the Kidstons were eating noon dinner. He appeared in the archway from the living room and removed his hat when he saw Lorraine at the table with the two men.

"It's done," Dancey said. "They're both under ground."

Vern looked up briefly. "All right."

"What about their gear?"

"Divvy it up."

"You could cast lots," Lorraine said.

Duane looked at her sternly. "That remark was in very poor taste."

Duane was looking at Vern now and not giving Lorraine time to reply.

"You mean to tell me you weren't present at their burial? Two men are murdered in your service and you don't even go out and read over their graves?"

"They were killed," Vern said. "Not in my service."

"All right." Duane couldn't hide his irritation. "No matter how it happened, it's proper for the commanding ... for the lead man to read Scripture over their graves."

"If the head man knows how to read," Lorraine said.

"I didn't know you were burying them right away." Duane's voice became grave. "Why didn't you tell me? I'd have read over them. I'd have considered it an honor. Two boys giving their lives defending—"

Vern's eyes stopped him. "That's enough of that. Duane, if I thought for a minute you sent those two over there—"

"I told you I didn't. They went on their own."

"Something else," Bill Dancey said. "Cable's moved his wife and kids into Denaman's."

Vern looked at him. "Who said so?"

"Man I sent to the store this morning. He saw the wagon and asked Luz about it. Luz says the woman and the kids are staying there, but Cable's going back to his place."

Vern rose from the table and walked around it toward Bill Dancey. He heard Duane say, "You'll run him out now; there's nothing to stop you. Vern, you hear me? You let me know when you're leaving because I want to be there." Vern did not reply or even look at Duane. Dancey turned and he followed him out through the long, beam-ceilinged, adobe-plastered living room, through the open double doors to the veranda that extended across the front of the house.

Dancey said, "What about their horses?"

"Put them in the remuda."

"Then what?"

"Then work for your money." As Dancey turned and started down the steps, Vern said, "Wait a minute." He moved against a support post and stood looking down at Dancey.

"How do you think he did it?"

"With a Colt and a rock," Dancey answered dryly.

"I asked you a question."

"And I don't know the answer you want." Dancey walked off, but he stopped within a few strides and looked back at Vern. "Why don't you ask Cable?"

"Maybe I will."

"With Joe Bob's brothers along?"

"He hit you, too, Bill. The first time you met him."

"Not that hard," Dancey said. He turned away.

Vern watched him continue on. So now it was even starting to bother Dancey, this fighting a lone man.

He was almost sure Cable had not murdered them.

He was sure Joe Bob and Royce had gone to him with drawn guns, but somehow Cable had outwitted them and had been forced to kill them. And that was the difficult fact to accept. That Cable was capable of killing them. That he could think calmly enough to outsmart them, to do that while having a wife and children to worry about; and then kill them, one of them with his hands, a rock, yes, but with his hands.

What kind of a man was this Cable?

What was his breaking point? If he had one. That was it, some people didn't have a breaking point. They stayed or they died, but they didn't give up.

And now, because he had handled Joe Bob and Royce, Cable's confidence would be bolstered and it would take more patience or more prying or more of whatever the hell it was going to take to get him off the Saber.

Kidston had made up his mind that the river land would be his, regardless of Cable or anyone else who cared to contest it with him. This was a simple act of will. He wanted the land because he needed it. His horses had grazed the lush river meadow for two years and he had come to feel that this land was rightfully his.

The news of Cable's return had caused him little concern. A Confederate soldier had come home with his family. Well, that was too bad for the Rebel. Somehow Cable had outmaneuvered three men and made them run. Luck, probably. But the Rebel wasn't staying, Kidston was certain of that.

He had worked too hard for too many years: starting on his own as a mustanger, breaking wild horses and selling them half-green to whoever needed a mount. Then hiring White Mountain Apache boys and gathering more mustangs each spring. He began selling to the Hatch & Hodges stage-line people. His operation expanded and he hired more men; then the war put an end to the Hatch & Hodges business. The war almost ruined him; yet it was the war that put him back in business, with a contract to supply remounts to the Union cavalry. He had followed the wild herds to the Saber River country and here he settled, rebuilding the old Toyopa place. He employed fourteen riders—twelve now—and looked forward to spending the rest of his life here.

During the second year of the war his brother Duane had written to him—first from their home in Gallipolis, Ohio, then from Washington after he had marched his own command there to join the Army of the Potomac—pleading with Vern to come offer his services to the Union army. That was like Duane, Vern had thought. Dazzled by the glory of it, by the drums and the uniforms, and probably not even remotely aware of what was really at stake. But it was at this time that Vern received the government contract for remounts. After that, joining the army was out of the question.

The next December Duane arrived with his daughter. Duane had not wanted to return to Gallipolis after having been relieved of his command. They had made him resign his commission because of incompetence or poor judgment or whatever shelling your own troops was called.

It had happened at Chancellorsville, during Duane's first and only taste of battle. His artillery company was thrown in to support Von Gilsa's exposed flank, south of the town and in the path of Stonewall Jackson's advance. When Von Gilsa's brigade broke and came running back, Duane opened fire on them and killed more Union soldiers than Jackson had been able to in his attack.

Duane, of course, gave his version. It was an understandable mistake. There had been no communication with Von Gilsa. They were running toward his position and he ordered the firing almost as a reflex action, the way a soldier is trained to react. It happened frequently; naturally mistakes were made in the heat of battle. It was expected. But Chancellorsville had been a Union defeat. That was why they forced him to resign his commission. A number of able commanders were relieved simply because the Army of the Potomac had suffered a setback.

Vern accepted his explanation and even felt somewhat sorry for him. But when Duane went on pretending he was a soldier and hired four new riders for his "scouts," as he called them, you could take just so much of that. What was it? Kidston's Guard, Scouts for Colonel J. H. Carleton, Military Department of Arizona. It was one thing to feel sympathy for Duane. It was another to let Duane assume so much importance just to soothe his injured pride.

And Lorraine, spoiled and bored and overly sure of herself. The worst combination you could find in a woman. Both she and her comic-opera officer of a father living under one roof. Still, it seemed there were some things you just had to put up with.

Though that didn't include a home-coming Confederate squeezing him off the river. Not after the years and the sweat, and breaking his back for every dollar he earned. . . .

That had been his reaction to Cable before he saw Cable face to face, before he talked to him. Since then, a gnawing doubt had crept into his mind. Cable had worked and sweated and fought, too. What about that?

Duane's logic at least simplified the question: Cable was an enemy of the Federal government in Federal territory. As such he had no rights. Take his land and good damn riddance.

"His family is *his* worry." Duane's words. "But in these times, Vern, and I'll testify to it, men with families are dying every day. We are a thousand miles from the fighting, but right here is an extension of the war. Sweep down on him! Drive him out! Burn him out if you have to!"

Still, Vern wished with all his strength that there was a way of driving Cable out without fighting him. He was not afraid of Cable. He respected him. And he respected his wife.

Vern found himself picturing the way Martha had walked out from the house with the shotgun under her arm. Cable was a lucky man to have a woman like that, a woman who could keep up with him and who had already given him three healthy children. A woman, Kidston felt, who thoroughly enjoyed being a woman and living with the man she loved.

He had thought that Luz Acaso was that kind exactly. In fact he had been sure of it. But ever since Janroe's coming she seemed a different person. That was something else to think about. Why would a woman as warm and openly affectionate as Luz change almost overnight? It concerned Janroe's presence, that much Kidston was sure of. But was Luz in love with him or mortally afraid of him? That was another question.

He heard steps behind him and looked over his shoulder to see Lorraine crossing the porch. She smiled at him pleasantly.

"Cabe makes you stop and think, doesn't he?"

"You're on familiar terms for only one meeting," Vern said.

"That's what his wife calls him." Lorraine watched her uncle lean against the support post. He looked away from her, out over the yard. "Don't you think that's unusual, a wife calling her husband by his last name?"

"Maybe that's what everybody calls him," Vern answered.

"Like calling you 'Kid.'" Lorraine smiled, then laughed. "No, I think she made up the name. I think it's her name for him. Hers only." Lorraine waited, letting the silence lengthen before asking, "What do you think of her?"

"I haven't thought."

"I thought you might have given Martha careful consideration."

"Why?"

"As a way of getting at her husband."

Vern looked at her now.

"What do you mean?"

Lorraine smiled. "You seem reluctant to use force. I doubt if you can buy him off. So what remains?"

"I'm listening."

"Strike at Cable from within."

"And what does that mean?"

Lorraine sighed. "Vern, you're never a surprise. You're as predictable as Duane, though you don't call nearly as much attention to yourself."

"Lorraine, if you have something to say——"

"I've said it. Go after him through Martha. Turn her against him. Break up his home. Then see how long he stays in that house."

"And if such a thing was possible——"

"It's very possible."

"How?"

"The other woman, Vern. How else?"

He watched her calmly. "And that's you."

She nodded once, politely. "Lorraine Kidston

67

as"—she paused—"I need a more provocative name for this role."

Vern continued to watch her closely. "And if he happens to love his wife?"

"Of course he loves her. Martha's an attractive woman if you like them strong, capable and somewhat on the plain side. But that has nothing to do with it. He's a man, Vern. And right now he's in that place all alone."

"You've got a wild mind," Vern said quietly. "I'd hate to live with it inside me." He turned away from her and walked down the steps and across the yard.

You shocked him, Lorraine thought amusedly, watching him go. But wait until the shock wears off. Wait until his conscience stops choking him. Vern would agree. He would have it understood that such methods went against his grain; but in the end he would agree. Lorraine was sure of it and she was smiling now.

Cable passed through the store and climbed the stairs to the bedroom where Martha was unpacking. He watched her removing linens and towels from the trunk at the foot of the bed, turning to place them in the open dresser drawer an arm's length away.

"The children will be in here?"

Martha looked up. "Clare and Dave. Sandy will sleep with me."

"With Luz here, I think you'll get along with Janroe all right."

"As long as the children eat in the kitchen."

"Martha, I'm sorry."

She saw his frown deepen the tightly drawn lines of his bruised face. "Someday I'm going to bite my tongue off. I shouldn't have said that."

"I can't blame you," Cable said.

"But it doesn't make it any easier."

"If you weren't here," Cable said, "it wouldn't even be possible." He moved close to her and put his arms around her as she straightened.

"I want to say something like 'It'll be over soon,' or 'Soon we'll be going back and there won't be any more waiting, any more holding your breath not knowing what's going to happen.' But I can't. I can't promise anything."

"Cabe, I don't need promises. Just so long as you're here with us, that's all we need."

"Do you want to leave? Right this minute get in the wagon and go back to Sudan?"

"You don't mean that."

"I do. You say it and we'll leave."

For a moment Martha was silent, standing close to him, close to his bruised cheekbone and his lips that were swollen and cut. "If we went back," Martha said, "I don't think you'd be an easy man to live with. You'd be nice and sometimes you'd smile, but I don't think you'd ever say very much, and it would be as if your mind was always on something else." A smile touched her mouth and showed warmly in her eyes. "We'll stay, Cabe."

She lifted her face to be kissed and when they looked at each other again she saw his smile and he seemed more at ease.

"Are you going back right now?"

"I have to talk to Janroe first." He kissed her again before stepping away. "I'll be up in a little while."

Janroe was sitting in the kitchen, his chair half turned from the table so that he could look directly out through the screen door. He paid no attention to Luz who was clearing the table, carrying the dishes to the wooden sink. He was thinking of the war, seeing himself during that afternoon of August 30, in the fields near Richmond, Kentucky.

If that day had never happened, or if it had happened differently; if he had not lost his arm—no, losing his arm was only an indirect reason for his being here. But it had led to this. It had been the beginning of the end.

After his wound had healed, eight months later, with his sleeve in his belt and even somewhat proud of it but not showing his pride, he had returned to his unit and served almost another full year before they removed him from active duty. His discharge was sudden. It came shortly after he had had the Yankee prisoners shot. They said he would have to resign his commission because of his arm; but he knew that was not the reason and he had pleaded with them to let him stay, pestering General Kirby

Smith's staff; but it came to nothing, and in the end he was sent home a civilian.

He had not told Cable about that year or about anything that had happened after August 30, after his arm was blown from his body. But Cable didn't have to know everything. Like soldiers before an engagement with the enemy—it was better not to tell them too much.

Stir them up, yes. Make them hate and be hungry to kill; but don't tell them things they didn't have to know, because that would start them thinking and soldiers in combat shouldn't think. You could scare them though. Sometimes that was all right. Get them scared for their own skins. Pour it into their heads that the enemy was ruthless and knew what he was doing and that he would kill them if they didn't kill' him. Beat them if they wouldn't fight!

God knows he had done that. He remembered again the afternoon near Richmond, coming out of the brush and starting across the open field toward the Union battery dug in on the pine ridge that was dark against the sky. He remembered screaming at his men to follow him. He remembered this, seeing himself now apart from himself, seeing Captain Edward Janroe waving a Dragoon pistol and shouting at the men who were still crouched at the edge of the brush. He saw himself running back toward them, then swinging the barrel at a man's head. The man ducked and scrambled out into the field. Others followed him; but two men still remained, down on their knees and staring up at him wide-eyed with fear. He shot one of them from close range, cleanly through the head; and the second man was out of the brush before he could swing the Dragoon on him.

Yes, you could frighten a man into action, scare him so that he was more afraid of you than the enemy. Janroe stopped.

Could that apply to Cable? Could Cable be scared into direct action?

He eased his position, looking at Luz who was standing at the sink with her back to him, then at the screen door again and the open sunlight beyond. He had given his mind the opportunity to reject these questions, to answer them negatively.

But why not? Why couldn't Cable be forced into killing the Kidstons? He had been a soldier—used to taking orders. No, he couldn't be ordered. But perhaps now, with his wife and children staying here, he would be more easily persuaded. Perhaps he could be forced into doing it. Somehow.

In Janroe's mind it was clear, without qualifying shades of meaning, that Vern and Duane Kidston were the enemy. In uniform or not in uniform they were Yankees and this was a time of war and they had to be killed. A soldier killed. An officer ordered his men to kill. That was what it was all about and that was what Janroe knew best.

They could close their eyes to this fact and believe they were acting as human beings—whatever the hell that meant in time of war—and relieve him of his command for what he did to those Yankee prisoners. They could send him out here to die of boredom; but he could still remember what a Yankee field piece did to his arm. He was still a soldier and he could still think like a soldier and act like a soldier and if his job was to kill—whether or not on the surface it was called gun-running—then he would kill.

He felt his chest rising and falling with his breathing and he glanced at Luz, calming himself then, inhaling and letting his breath out slowly.

Still, an officer used strategy. He fought with his eyes open; not rushing blindly, unless there was no other way to do it. An officer studied a situation and used what means he had at hand. If the means was a brigade or only one man, he used that means to the best of his ability.

Janroe looked up as Cable entered the kitchen. He glanced at Luz then, catching her eye, and the girl dried her hands and stepped out through the back door.

"I've been waiting for you," Janroe said.

"I was with my wife." Cable hesitated. "We're grateful for what you're doing."

"I guess you are."

Cable sat down, removing his hat and wiping his forehead with the back of his hand. "Martha will be glad to help out with the housekeeping, and she'll keep the children out from under your feet."

"I took that for granted," Janroe said.

"We'll be out of your way as soon as I settle this business with the Kidstons."

"And how long will that take?"

"Look, we'll leave right now if you want."

"You lose your temper too easily," Janroe said. "I was asking you a simple question."

Cable looked at him, then at his own hand curling the brim of his hat. "I don't know; it's up to the Kidstons."

"It could be up to you, if you wanted it to be."

"If I kill them."

"You didn't have any trouble last night."

"Last night two men came to my home," Cable said. "My family was in danger and I didn't have any choice. Though I'll tell you this: I didn't mean to kill them. That just happened. If Vern and Duane come threatening my home, then I could kill them too because I wouldn't be trying to kill them; I'd be trying to protect my home and my family, and there's a difference. When you say kill them, just go out and do it; that's something else."

Janroe was sitting back in his chair, his hand idly rubbing the stump of his arm; but now he leaned forward. His hand went to the edge of the table and he pushed the chair back.

"We could argue that point for a long time." He stood up then. "Come on, I'll show you something."

Cable hesitated, then rose and followed Janroe through the store and out to the loading platform. The children were at one end, stopped in whatever they were playing or pretending by the sudden appearance of Janroe. They looked at their father, wanting to go to him, but they seemed to sense a threat in approaching Janroe and they remained where they were.

Janroe said, "Tell them to go around back."

"They're not bothering anything." Cable moved toward the children.

"Listen," Janroe said patiently, "just get rid of them for a while—all right?"

He waited while Cable talked to the three children. Finally they moved off, taking their time and looking back as they turned the corner of the adobe. When they were out of sight, Janroe went down the stairs and, to Cable's surprise, ducked under the loading platform.

Cable followed, lowering his head to step through the cross timbers into the confining dimness. He moved with hunched shoulders the few steps to where Janroe was removing the padlock from a door in the adobe foundation.

"This used to be a storeroom," Janroe muttered. He pushed the door open and moved aside. "Go on; there's a lantern in there."

Cable hesitated, then stepped past him, glancing back to make sure Janroe was coming.

Janroe followed, saying, "Feel along the wall, you'll find it."

Cable turned, raising his left hand. He heard the door swing closed and he was in abrupt total darkness.

He heard Janroe's steps and felt him move close behind him. Too close! Cable tried to turn, reaching for the Walker at the same time; but his hand twisted behind him and pulled painfully up between his shoulder blades. He tried to lunge forward, tried to twist himself free, but as he did Janroe's foot scissored about his ankles and Cable fell forward, landing heavily on the hard-packed floor with Janroe on top of him.

Chapter Four

Now there was silence.

With Janroe's full weight on top of him and the cool hardness of the floor flat against his cheek, Cable did not move. He felt Janroe's chest pressing heavily against his back. His right arm, twisted and held between their bodies, sent tight, muscle-straining pain up into his shoulder. Janroe had pulled his own hand free as they struck the floor. It gripped the handle of Cable's revolver, then tightened on it as the boards creaked above them.

Faint footsteps moved through the store and faded again into silence. Cable waited, listening, and making his body relax even with the weight pressing against him. He was thinking: It could be Martha, gone out to call the children. Martha not twenty feet away.

He felt the Walker slide from its holster. Janroe's weight shifted, grinding heavily into his back. The cocking action of the Walker was loud and close to him before the barrel burrowed into the pit of his arm.

"Don't spoil it," Janroe whispered.

They waited. In the darkness, in the silence, neither spoke. Moments later the floor creaked again and the soft footsteps crossed back through the store. Cable let his breath out slowly.

Janroe murmured, "I could have pulled the trigger. A minute ago I was unarmed; but just then I could have killed you."

Cable said nothing. Janroe's elbow pressed into his back. The pressure eased and he felt Janroe push himself to his feet. Still Cable waited. He heard Janroe adjust a lantern. A match scratched down the wall. Its flare died almost to nothing, then abruptly the floor in front of Cable's face took form. His eyes raised from his own shadow and in the dull light he saw four oblong wooden cases stacked against the wall close in front of him.

"Now you can get up," Janroe said.

Cable rose. He stretched the stiffness from his body, working his shoulder to relieve the sharp muscle strain, his eyes returning to Janroe now and seeing the Walker in Janroe's belt, tight against his stomach.

"Did you prove something by that?"

"I want you to know," Janroe said, "that I'm not just passing the time of day."

"There's probably an easier way."

"No." Janroe shook his head slowly. "I want you to realize that I could have killed you. That I'd do it in a minute if I thought I had to. I want that to sink into your head."

"You wouldn't have a reason."

"The reason's behind you. Four cases of Enfield rifles. They're more important than any one man's life. More important than yours—"

Cable stopped him. "You're not making much sense."

"Or more important than the lives of Vern and Duane Kidston," Janroe finished. "Does that make sense?"

"My hunting license." Cable watched him thoughtfully. "Isn't that what you called it? If I was in the gun-running business, I could kill them with a clear conscience."

"I'll tell it to you again," Janroe said. "If you worked for me, I'd order you to kill them."

"I remember."

"But it still hasn't made any impression."

"I told you a little while ago, now it's up to the Kidstons."

"All right, what do you think they're doing right this minute?"

"Maybe burying their dead," Cable said. "And realizing something."

"And Joe Bob's brothers—do you think they're just going to bury him and forget all about it?"

"That's something else," Cable said.

"No it isn't, because Vern will use them. He'll sic them on you like a pair of mad dogs."

"I don't think so. I've got a feeling Vern's the kind of man who has to handle something like this himself, his own way."

"And you'd bet the lives of your family on it," Janroe said dryly.

"It's Vern's move, not mine."

"Like a chess game."

"Look," Cable said patiently. "You're asking me to shoot the man down in cold blood and that's what I can't do. Not for any reason."

"Even though you left your family and rode a thousand miles to fight the Yankees." Janroe watched him closely, making sure he held Cable's attention.

"Now you're home and you got Yankees right in your front yard. But now, for some reason, it's different. They're supplying cavalry horses to use against the same boys you were in uniform with. They're using your land to graze those horses. But now it's different. Now you sit and wait because it's the Yankees' turn to move."

"A lot of things don't sound sensible," Cable said, "when you put them into words."

"Or when you cover one ear," Janroe said. "You don't hear the guns or the screams and the moans of the wounded. You even have yourself believing the war's over."

"I told you once, it's over as far as I'm concerned."

Janroe nodded. "Yes, you've told me and you've told yourself. Now go tell Vern Kidston and his brother."

End it, Cable thought. Tell him to shut up and mind his own business. But he thought of Martha and the children. They were here in the safety of this man's house, living here now because Janroe had agreed to it. He was obligated to Janroe, and the sudden awareness of it checked him, dissolving the bald, blunt words that were clear in his mind and almost on his tongue.

He said simply, "I don't think we're getting anywhere."

Janroe's expression remained coldly impassive; still his eyes clung to Cable. He watched him intently, almost as if he were trying to read Cable's thoughts.

"You might think about it though," Janroe said. His eyes dropped briefly. He pulled the Walker from his waist and handed it butt-forward to Cable.

"Within a few days, I'm told, Bill Dancey and the rest of them will start bringing all the horses in from pasture. That means Duane and maybe even Vern will be home alone. Just the two of them there." Janroe lifted the lantern from the wall. Before blowing it out, he added, "You might think about that, too."

They moved out of the cellar into the abrupt sun glare of the yard, and there Janroe waited while Cable went inside to tell Martha good-by. Within a few minutes Cable reappeared. Janroe watched him kneel down to kiss his children; he watched him mount the sorrel and ride out. He watched him until he was out of sight, and still he lingered in the yard, staring out through the sun haze to the willows that lined the river.

He isn't mad enough, Janroe was thinking. And Vern seems to want to wait and sweat him out. If he waits, Cable waits and nothing happens. And it will go on like this until you bring them together. You know that, don't you? Somehow you have to knock their heads together.

Manuel Acaso reached Cable's house in the late evening. The sky was still light, with traces of sun reflection above the pine slope, but the glare was gone and the trees had darkened and seemed more silent.

Manuel moved through the streaked shadows of the aspen grove, through the scattered pale-white trees, hearing only the sound of his own horse in the leaves. He stopped at the edge of the trees, his eyes on the silent, empty-appearing adobe; then he moved on.

Halfway across the yard he called out, "Paul!"

Cable parted the hanging willow branches with the barrel of the Spencer and stepped into the open. Manuel was facing the house, sitting motionless in the saddle with his body in profile as Cable approached, his face turned away and his eyes on the door of the house.

He looks the same, Cable thought. Perhaps heavier, but not much; and he still looks as if he's part of the saddle and the horse, all three of them one, even when he just sits resting.

Softly he said, "Manuel—"

The dark lean face in the shadow of the straw hat turned to Cable without a trace of surprise, but with a smile that was real and warmly relaxed. His eyes raised to the willows, then dropped to Cable again.

"Still hiding in trees," Manuel said. "Like when the Apache would come. Never be where they think you are."

Cable was smiling. "We learned that, Manolo."

"Now to be used on a man named Kidston," Manuel said. "Did you think I was him coming?"

"You could have been."

"Always something, uh?"

"Why didn't you run him when he first came?"

Manuel shrugged. "Why? It's not my land."

"You skinny Mexican, you were too busy running something else."

The trace of a smile left Manuel's face. "I didn't think Janroe would have told you so soon."

"You haven't seen him this evening?"

"No, I didn't stop."

"But you knew I was here."

"A man I know visited the store yesterday. Luz told him," Manuel said. "I almost stopped to see Martha and the little kids, but I thought, no, talk to him first, about Janroe."

"He wants me to join you, but I told him I had my own troubles."

"He must see something in you." Manuel leaned forward, resting his arms one over the other on the saddle horn, watching Cable closely. "What do you think of him?"

Cable hesitated. "I'm not sure."

"He told you how he came and how he's helping with the guns?"

"That he was in the war before and wounded."

"Do you believe him?"

"I don't have a reason not to. But I don't understand him."

"That's the way I felt about him; and still do."

"Did you check on him?"

"Sure. I asked the people I work with. They said of course he's all right, or he wouldn't have been sent here."

Looking up at Manuel, Cable smiled. It was good to see him, good to talk to him again, in the open or anywhere, and for the first time in three days Cable felt more sure of himself. The feeling came over him quietly with the calm, unhurried look of this man who lounged easily in his saddle and seemed a part of it—this thin-faced, slim-bodied man who looked like a boy and always would, who had worked his cattle with him and fought the Apache with him and helped him build his home. They had learned to know each other well, and there was much between them that didn't have to be spoken.

"Do you feel someone watching you?"

"This standing in the open," Manuel nodded. "Like being naked."

"We'd better go somewhere else."

"In the trees." Manuel smiled.

He took his horse to the barn and came back, walking with a slow, stiff-legged stride, his hand lightly on the Colt that was holstered low on his right side, holding it to his leg. He followed Cable in to the willows. Then, sitting down next to him at the edge of the cutbank, Manuel noticed the horse herd far out in the meadow beyond the river.

"You let Vern's horses stay?"

"I ran them once," Cable said. "Duane brought them back."

"So you run them again."

"Tomorrow. You want to come?"

"Tonight I'm back to my gun business."

Denaman, Cable thought. The old man's face appeared suddenly in his mind with the mention of the gun-running. He told Manuel what Janroe had said about John Denaman's death. That he was worried about his business. "But I suppose that meant worried about the guns," Cable said. "Having to sit on them and act natural."

"I think the man was just old," Manuel said. "I think he would have died anyway. Perhaps this gun business caused him to die a little sooner, but not much sooner."

"I'm sorry—"

"Thank you," Manuel said, with understanding, as if Denaman had been his own father.

"At first," Cable said, "I couldn't picture John fooling

79

with something like this—living out here, far away from the war."

"Why?" Manuel's eyebrows rose. "You lived here and you went to fight."

"It seems different."

"Because he was old? John could have had the same feeling you did."

"I suppose."

"Sure, and I think you going off to war, and the other people he knew who went, convinced him he had to do something to help. Since he couldn't become a soldier he did this with the guns."

"Did he talk to you about it first?"

Manuel shook his head. "There were already guns under the store when I found out. John got into it through some man he knew who lives in Hidalgo. He didn't want me to help, said I had no part in it. But I told him if he believed in what he was doing then so did I, so why waste our breath over it."

"Do you believe in it?"

"I believed in John; that's enough."

"But what about now?"

"He started it," Manuel said. "I'll finish it, with or without the help of this man who's so anxious to kill."

"Something else," Cable said. "Janroe told me that John was worried about Luz. That she was keeping company with Vern, and John didn't like it."

Manuel nodded. "She was seeing him often before Janroe came. Sometimes it bothered me, Vern being around; but John said, no, that was good, let him sit up there in the parlor with Luz. If we sneaked around and stayed to ourselves, John said, then people would suspect things. . . . So I don't think he was worried about Vern Kidston. If anything, John liked him. They talked well together; never about the war but about good things. . . . No, Janroe is wrong about that part. He figured it out himself and maybe it made sense to him, but he's wrong."

"Luz stopped seeing Vern?"

"Right after Janroe came."

"Do you know why?"

"I think because she was afraid Janroe would kill

him, or try to, and if it happened at the store it would be because of her." Manuel paused. "Does that make sense?"

"I suppose. Since she knew Janroe and Vern were on opposite sides."

"Luz is afraid of him and admits it," Manuel said. "She says she has a feeling about him and sees him in dreams as a *nagual*, a man who is able to change himself into something else. A man who is two things at the same time."

"He could be two different people," Cable said, nodding. "He could be what he tells you and he could be what he is, or what he is thinking. I don't know. I don't even know how to talk to him. He wants me to work for him and kill Vern and Duane because of what they're doing."

Manuel stared. "He asked me to do that, months ago."

"What did you tell him?"

"To go to hell."

"That's what I wanted to say," Cable said. "But now Martha and the kids are living in his house and I have to go easy with him. But he keeps insisting and arguing it and after a while I run out of things to tell him."

In the dimness, Manuel leaned closer, putting his hand on Cable's arm. "Do you want to find out more about this Janroe?"

"How?"

"I'll take you to the man I work for. John's friend from Hidalgo. He can tell you things."

"I don't know—"

"You were at the war and you'd understand what he says about Janroe. You'd be able to ask questions."

"Maybe I'd better." Cable's tone was low, thoughtful.

"Listen, you're worried about your land; I know that. But after this I'll help you and we'll run these Kidstons straight to hell if you say it."

"All right," Cable nodded. "We'll talk to your man."

It was still sky-red twilight when they rode out, but full dark by the time they passed the store, keeping to the west side of the river and high up on the slope so they wouldn't be heard.

Martha stood at the sink, taking her time with the breakfast dishes, making it last because she wasn't sure what she would do after this. Perhaps ask Luz if she could help with something else. Luz, not Mr. Janroe. But even if there was something to be done, Luz would shake her head no, Martha was sure of that. So what would she do then? Perhaps go outside with the children.

Her gaze rose from the dishwater to the window and she saw her children playing in the back yard: Davis and Sandy pushing stick-trains over the hard-packed ground and making whistle sounds; Clare sitting on a stump, hunched over her slate with the tip of her tongue showing in the corner of her mouth.

They're used to not seeing him, Martha thought. But you're not used to it, not even after two and a half years. And now he seems farther away than before.

That was a strange thing. She had waited for Cable during the war knowing he would come home, knowing it and believing it, because she prayed hard and allowed herself to believe nothing else. Now he was within one hour's ride, but the distance between them seemed greater than when he had served with General Forrest. And now, too, there was an uncertainty inside of her. Because you haven't had time to think about it, she thought. Or not think about it. This time you haven't gotten used to not thinking anything will happen to him.

For a moment the thought angered her. She had things to do at home. She had a family to care for, husband and children, but she stood calmly waiting and washing dishes in another person's house, away from her husband again, and again faced with the tiring necessity of telling herself everything would be all right.

Was it worth it?

If it wasn't, was anything worth waiting or fighting for?

And she thought, if you don't have the desire to fight or wait for something, there's no reason for being on earth.

That's very easy to say. Now wash the dishes and live with it. Martha smiled then. No, she told herself, it was simply a question of stubbornness or resignation. If you ran away from one trouble, you would probably run into another. So face the first one, the important one, and get used to it. She remembered Cable saying, years before, "We've taken all there is to take. Nothing will make us leave this place."

And perhaps you can believe that, just as you knew and believed he would come home from the war, Martha thought. So put on the big-smiling mask again. Even if it makes you gag.

But I'm tired, Martha thought, not smiling now. Perhaps you can keep the mask on only so long before it suffocates you.

She glanced over her shoulder as Luz entered the kitchen.

"I think Mr. Janroe is going out," Luz said. She pulled a towel from a hook above the sink and began drying dishes. "He's in the store, but dressed to go out."

"Where would he be going?" Martha asked.

"I don't know. Sometimes he just rides off."

"Would it have anything to do with the guns?"

Luz looked at her. "You know?"

"Of course. Don't you think Paul would have told me?"

"I wasn't sure."

"Luz, do you have anything to do with it?"

The girl nodded. "On the day the guns are to arrive, I ride down to Hidalgo in the afternoon. That night I return an hour ahead of them seeing that the way is clear. Manuel follows, doing the same. Then the guns come."

"Are you due to go again soon—or shouldn't I ask that?"

"It doesn't matter." The girl shrugged. "Tomorrow I go again."

"Aren't you afraid?"

"Not when I'm away from here."

"But you're afraid of Mr. Janroe," Martha said. "I'm sure of that. Why, Luz?"

"You don't know him or you wouldn't ask that."

"I know he's gruff. Hardly what you'd call a gentleman."

"No." Luz shook her head solemnly. She glanced at the doorway to the main room before saying, "It isn't something you see in him."

"Has he ever . . . made advances?"

"No, it isn't like that either," the girl said. "It's something you feel. Like an awareness of evil. As if his soul was so smeared with stains of sin you were aware of a foulness about him that could almost be smelled."

"Luz, to your knowledge the man hasn't done a thing wrong."

"The feeling is a kind of knowledge itself."

"But it isn't something you can prove, is it?" Martha stood with her hands motionless in the dishwater, her full attention on Luz. "What if suddenly you realize that all you've said couldn't possibly be true, that it's all something out of a dream or—"

"Listen, I did dream about him! A number of times before, then again last night." The girl's eyes went to the main room and back again.

"I saw an animal in the dream, like a small wolf or a coyote, and it was slinking along in the moonlight. Then, in front of it, there was a chicken. The chicken was feeding on the ground and before it could raise its head, the animal was on it and tearing it apart with its teeth and eating it even while the chicken was still alive. I watched, cold with fear, but unable to move. And as I watched, the animal began to change.

"It was still on its haunches facing me, still eating and smeared with the blood of the chicken. First it's hind legs became human legs; then its body became the clothed body of a man. Then the face began to change, the jaw and the nose and the chin. The teeth were still those of an animal and he had no forehead and his eyes and head were still like an animal's. He was looking at me with blood on his mouth and on his hand . . . on the one hand that he had. And at that moment I ran from him screaming. I knew it was the face of Mr. Janroe."

"Luz, you admit it's a dream—"

"Listen, that isn't all of it." Luz glanced toward the main room again. "I awoke in a sweat and with a thirst burning the inside of my throat. So I left my bed and went down for a drink of water. The big room was dark, but at once I saw that a lamp was burning in here. I came to the door, I looked into this room, and I swear on my mother's grave that my heart stopped beating when I saw him."

"Mr. Janroe?"

Luz nodded quickly. "He was sitting at the table holding a piece of meat almost to his mouth and his eyes were on me, not as if he'd looked up as I appeared, but as if he'd been watching me for some time. I saw his eyes and the hand holding the meat, just as in the dream, and I ran. I don't know if I screamed, but I remember wanting to scream and running up the stairs and locking my door."

Martha dried her hands on her apron. She smiled at Luz gently and put her hand on the girl's arm.

"Luz, there isn't anything supernatural about a man eating with his fingers."

"You didn't see him." Luz stopped. Her eyes were on the doorway again and a moment later Janroe appeared. Martha glanced at him, then at Luz again as the girl suddenly turned and pushed through the screen door.

Janroe came into the kitchen. He was holding his hat and wearing a coat, but the coat was open and Martha noticed the butt of a Colt beneath one lapel in a shoulder holster. Another Colt was on his hip.

"Did I interrupt something?"

"Nothing important." Martha turned from the sink to face him. "You're going out?"

"I thought I would." He watched her with an expression of faint amusement. "Wondering if I'm going to see your husband?"

"Yes, I was."

"I might see him."

"If you're going that way, would you mind stopping by the house?"

"Why?"

"Why do you think, Mr. Janroe?"

"Maybe he's not so anxious to let you know what he's doing."

Now a new side of him, Martha thought wearily. She said nothing.

"I mean, considering how he dropped you here and ran off so quick." Janroe hooked his hat on the back of the nearest chair. Unhurriedly he started around the table, saying now, "A man is away from his wife for two years

85

or more, then soon as he gets home he leaves her again. What kind of business is that?"

Martha watched him still coming toward her. "We know the reason, Mr. Janroe."

"The reason he gives. Worried about his wife and kids."

"What other reason is there?"

"It wouldn't be my business to know."

"You seem to be making it your business."

"I was just wondering if you believed him."

He was close to her now. Martha stood unmoving, feeling the wooden sink against her back. "I believe him," she said calmly. "I believe anything he tells me."

"Did he tell you he led a saintly life the years he was away?"

"I never questioned him about it."

"Want me to tell you what a man does when he's away from home?"

"And even if I said no—"

"They have a time for themselves," Janroe went on. "They carry on like young bucks with the first smell of spring. Though they expect their wives to sit home and be as good as gold."

"You know this from experience?"

"I've seen them." His voice was low and confiding. "Some of them come home with the habit of their wild ways still inside them, and they go wandering off again."

He watched her closely, his head lowered and within inches of hers. "Then there's some women who aren't fooled by it and they say, 'If he can fool around and have a time, then so can I.' Those women do it, too. They start having a time for themselves and it serves their husbands right."

Martha did not move. She was looking at him, at his heavy mustache and the hard, bony angles of his face, feeling the almost oppressive nearness of him. She said nothing.

Janroe asked, almost a whisper, "You know what I mean?"

"If I were to tell my husband what you just said," Martha answered quietly, "I honestly believe he would kill you."

Janroe's expression did not change. "I don't think so. Your husband needs me. He needs a place for you and the kids to stay."

"Are you telling me that I'm part of the agreement between you and my husband?"

"Well now, nothing so blunt as all that." Janroe smiled. "We're white men."

"We'll be out of here within an hour," Martha said coldly.

"Now wait a minute. You don't kid very well, do you?"

"Not about that."

He backed away from her, reaching for his hat. "I don't even think you know what I was talking about."

"Let's say that I didn't," Martha said. "For your sake."

Janroe shrugged. "You think whatever you want." He put his hat on and walked out. In front of the store, he mounted a saddled buckskin and rode off.

He could still see the calm expression of Martha Cable's face as he forded the shallow river, as he kicked the buckskin up the bank and started across the meadow that rolled gradually up into the pines that covered the crest of the slope. Then he was spurring, running the buckskin, crossing the sweep of meadow, in the open sunlight now with the hot breeze hissing past his face. But even then Martha was before him.

She stared at him coldly. And the harder he ran—holding the reins short to keep the buckskin climbing, feeling the brute strength of the horse's response, hearing the hoofs and the wind and trying to be aware of nothing else—the more he was aware of Martha's contempt for him.

Some time later, following the trail that ribboned through the pines, the irritating feeling that he had made a fool of himself began to subside. It was as if here in the silence, in the soft shadows of the pines, he was hidden from her eyes.

He told himself to forget about her. The incident in the kitchen had been a mistake. He had seen her and started talking and one thing had led to another; not planned, just something suddenly happening that moment.

He would have to be more careful. She was an attractive woman and her husband was miles away, but there were matters at hand more important than Martha Cable. She would wait until later, when there were no Kidstons . . . and no Paul Cable.

Still, telling himself this, her calmness and the indifference grated on his pride and he was sure that she had held him off because of his missing arm, because he was something repulsive to her. Only part of a man.

He jerked his mind back to the reason he was here. First, to talk to Cable, to hammer away at him until he consented to go after the Kidstons. Then, to scout around and see what was going on.

The latter had become a habit: riding this ridge trail, then bearing off toward the Kidston place and sometimes approaching within view of the house. He did this every few days and some times at night, because if you kept your eyes open you learned things. Like Duane's habit of sitting on the veranda at night—perhaps every night—for a last cigar. Or Vern visiting his grazes once a week and sometimes not returning until the next morning. But always there had been people around the house while Duane sat and smoked on the veranda; and almost invariably Vern made his inspections with Bill Dancey along. Knowing that Kidston's riders would be off on a horse gather in a few days was the same kind of useful intelligence to keep in mind. He had already told Cable about the riders being away. Perhaps he would tell him everything—every bit of information he knew about Vern and Duane Kidston. Lay it all out on the table and make it look easy.

High on the slope, but now even with Cable's house, Janroe reined in. There was no sign of life below. No sounds, no movement, no chimney smoke. But Cable could still be home, Janroe decided.

Then, descending the path, keeping his eyes on the shingled roof and the open area of the front yard, he began to think: But what if he isn't home?

Then you talk to him another time.

No, wait. What if he isn't home and isn't even close by?

Reaching the back of the adobe, he sat for a moment, listening thoughtfully to the silence.

And what if something happened to his house while he was away? Janroe began to feel the excitement of it building inside of him.

But be careful, he thought.

He rode around to the front and called Cable's name.

No answer.

He waited; called again, but still the house stood silent and showed no signs of life.

Janroe reined the buckskin around and crossed the yard to the willows. His gaze went to the horse herd out on the meadow and he studied the herd for some moments. No, Cable wasn't there. No one was.

He was about to turn back to the house, but he hesitated. No one anywhere. What does that say?

No, it's too good. When a thing looks too good there's something wrong with it. Still, he knew that all at once he was looking at an almost foolproof way to jab Cable into action. He sat motionless, looking at the horse herd, making sure no riders were out beyond the farthest grazing horses, and thinking it all over carefully.

Would he be suspected? No. He'd tell Martha and Luz he went to Fort Buchanan on business and no one was home when he passed here. He could even head up toward Buchanan, spend the night on the trail and double back to the store in the morning.

But what if someone came while he was in the house? What if Cable came home?

You either do it or you don't do it, but you don't think about it any more!

It was decided then. He returned to the adobe, swung down as he reached the ramada, and pushed open the front door.

Inside, in the dim closeness of the room, an urgency came over him and he told himself to hurry, to get it over with and get out.

From the stove he picked up a frying pan, went to the kitchen cupboards, opened them and swung the pan repeatedly into the shelves of dishes until not a cup or a plate remained in one piece. With a chair he smashed down the stove's chimney flue. A cloud of soot puffed out and filtered through the room as he dragged the comforter and blankets from the bed. He emptied the kitchen drawers then, turning them upside down; found a carving knife and used it to slash open the mattress and pillows still on the bed.

Enough?

He was breathing heavily from the exertion, from the violence of what had taken him no more than a minute. Hesitating now, his eyes going over the room, he again felt the urgent need to be out of here.

Enough.

He went out brushing soot from his coat, mounted and rode directly across the yard and forded the river. He stopped long enough to convince himself that no riders had joined the Kidston herd since his last look at it. Then he rode on, spurring across the meadow now, pointing for the east slope and not until he was in the piñon, beginning the steep climb up through the trees, did he look back and across to Cable's house. Not until then did he take the deep breath he had wanted to take in the house to make himself relax.

You've pushed him now, Janroe told himself, hearing the words calmly, but still feeling the excitement, the tension, tight through his body.

You just busted everything wide open.

It was evening, but not yet dark, a silent time with the trees standing black and thick-looking and the sky streaked with red shades of sun reflection. A whole day had passed and Cable was returning home.

He had already skirted the store, wanting to see Martha but wanting more to avoid Janroe, and now he was high up in the shadows and the silence of the pines, following the horse trail along the ridge.

He would talk to Janroe another time, after he had thought this out and was sure he knew what to say to him.

This morning he had talked to a man, a small old man who was perhaps in his sixties with a graying beard and a mustache that was tobacco-stained yellow about his mouth. Denaman's friend from Hidalgo. In the dimness of the adobe room, and with the early morning sounds of the village outside, the man seemed too old or too small or too fragile to do whatever he was doing.

But he asked Manuel Acaso questions about Cable,

then looked at Cable and asked more questions; and it was his eyes that convinced Cable that the man was not too old or too thin or too frail. Brown eyes—Cable would remember them—that were gentle and perhaps kind; but they were not smiling eyes. They were the eyes of a patient, soft-spoken man who would show little more than mild interest at anything he saw or heard.

He was willing enough to talk about Janroe once he was sure of Cable, and he made no attempt to hide facts or try to justify Janroe's actions. He spoke slowly, carefully, as if he had memorized the things he was saying. . . .

Edward Janroe, Cable learned, was a native of Florida, born in St. Augustine a few years before the outbreak of the second Seminole war, and had lived there most of his early life. Almost nothing was known of Janroe during this period; not until he joined the army in 1854. From then on his life was on record.

In 1858, a sergeant by this time, Janroe was court-martialed for knifing a fellow soldier in a tavern fight. The man died and Janroe was sentenced to six years of hard labor at the Fort Marion military prison. He was well into his third year of it when the war broke out. It saved him from completing his sentence.

With a volunteer company from St. Augustine, Janroe traveled to Winchester, Virginia—this during the summer of 1861—and was assigned to the 10th Virginia Infantry, part of General Edmund Kirby Smith's forces. Strangely enough, despite his prison record, but undoubtedly because of his experience, Janroe was commissioned a full lieutenant of infantry.

A year later, and now a captain, Janroe lost his arm at the battle of Richmond, Kentucky. He was sent to the army hospital at Knoxville, spent seven months there, and was discharged sometime in March, 1863.

But Janroe didn't go home. He learned that Kirby Smith had been made commander of the Trans-Mississippi Department, headquartered at Shreveport, Louisiana, and that's where Janroe went. In the early part of April he was reinstated with the rank of lieutenant and served under Dick Taylor, one of Kirby Smith's field generals.

Up to this point Cable had listened in silence.

"He didn't tell me that."

"I don't care what he told you," the bearded man said. "He served under Taylor in the fighting around Alexandria and Opelousas."

But not for long. He was with Taylor less than two months when he was discharged for good. He was told that he had given enough of himself and deserved retirement. The real reason: his wild disregard for the safety of his men, throwing them into almost suicidal charges whenever he made contact with the enemy. This, and the fact that he refused to take a prisoner. During his time with Taylor, Janroe was responsible for having some one hundred and twenty Union prisoners lined up and shot.

Janroe pleaded his case all the way to Kirby Smith's general staff—he was a soldier and soldiering was his life; but as far as every one of them was concerned, Janroe was unfit for active duty and immediately relieved of his command.

Janroe returned to St. Augustine, then in the hands of Federal forces. Through a man he had known there before, he made contact with Confederate Intelligence agents and went to work for them. And eventually—in fact after well over a year in Florida—he was sent to Mexico. There he was given his present assignment.

"I can see why he didn't tell me everything," Cable said.

The bearded man nodded. "Naturally."

Cable watched him. "What do you think of Janroe?"

"He's a hard man to know."

"But what do you think?"

"I don't care for his kind, if that's what you mean."

"Yet you have him working for you."

"Mr. Cable," the bearded man said, "Janroe seems to have one aim in life. To see the South win the war."

"Or to see more Yankees killed."

"What's the difference?"

"You know what I mean."

"I know he's moved over two thousand rifles through the store since coming here," the bearded man said.

"And now he wants to kill two men who aren't even in the war."

"Well, I wonder if you can blame him," the bearded

man said, somewhat wearily now. "A man is sent to war and taught how to kill; but after, the unlearning of it is left up to him."

"Except that Janroe knew how to kill before he went to war," Cable said.

So you'll wait, Cable thought now, and wonder about Janroe and wonder when Vern will make his move, while you try to stay calm and keep yourself from running away.

He was perhaps a mile from his house, passing through a clearing in the pines, when he saw the two riders down in the meadow, saw them for one brief moment before they entered the willows at the river.

Cable waited. When the riders did not come out of the trees on this side of the river he dismounted, took his field glasses and Spencer from the saddle and made his way carefully down through the pines on foot. Between fifty and sixty yards from the base of the slope he reached an outcropping of rock that fell steeply, almost abruptly, the rest of the way down. Here Cable went on his stomach. He nosed the Spencer through a V in the warm, sand-colored rocks and put the field glasses to his eyes.

He recognized Lorraine Kidston at once. She stood by her horse, looking down at a stooped man drinking from the edge of the water. When he rose, turning to the girl, wiping his mouth with the back of his hand, Cable saw that it was Vern Kidston.

Two hundred yards away, but with them, close to them through the field glasses, Cable watched. He studied Vern standing heavily with his hands on his hips, his shoulders slightly stooped and his full mustache giving his face a solemn, almost sad expression. Vern spoke little. Lorraine seemed to be doing the talking. Lorraine smiling blandly, shrugging, standing with one hand on her hip and gesturing imperiously with the other.

She stopped. For a moment neither of them spoke: Vern thoughtful; Lorraine watching them. Then Vern nodded, slowly, resignedly, and Lorraine was smiling again. Now she moved to her horse. Vern helped her up. She rode off at once, heading north out into the meadow, and did not look back. Vern watched her, standing motionless with his hands hanging at his sides now.

He was close, his hat, his mustache, his shirt, his gun belt, his hands, all in detail. Then the glasses lowered and Vern Kidston was a small dark figure two hundred yards away.

There he is, Cable thought. Waiting for you.

He put the field glasses aside and took the solid, compact, balanced weight of the Spencer, his hands under it lightly and the stock snugly against the groove of his shoulder.

There he is.

It would be easy, Cable thought. He knew that most of the waiting and the wondering and the wanting to run would be over by just squeezing the trigger. Doing it justifiably, he told himself.

And it isn't something you haven't done before.

There had been the two Apaches he had knocked from their horses as they rode out of the river trees and raced for his cattle. He had been lying on this same slope, up farther, closer to the house and with a Sharps rifle, firing and loading and firing again and seeing the two Chiricahua Apaches pitch from their running horses, not even knowing what had killed them.

And there had been another time. More like this one, though he had not been alone then. Two years ago. Perhaps two years almost to the day. In northern Alabama. . . .

It had happened on the morning of the fifth day, after they had again located the Yankee raider Abel Streight and were closing with him, preparing to tear another bite out of his exhausted flank.

He lay in the tall grass, wet and chilled by the rain that had been falling almost all night; now in the gray mist of morning with a shivering trooper huddled next to him, not speaking, and the rest of the patrol back a few hundred yards with the horses, waiting for the word to be passed to them. For perhaps an hour he lay like this with his glasses on the Union picket, a 51st Indiana Infantryman. The Yankee had been closer than Vern Kidston was now: across a stream and somewhat below them, crouched down behind a log, his rifle straight up past his head and shoulder. He was in plain view, facing the stream, the peak of his forage cap wet-shining and low over his eyes;

but his eyes were stretched wide open, Cable knew, because of the mist and the silence and because he was alone on picket duty a thousand miles from home. He's wondering if he will ever see Indiana again, Cable had thought. Wondering if he will ever see his home and his wife and his children. He's old enough to have a family. But he hasn't been in it long, or he wouldn't be showing himself.

I can tell you that you won't go home again, Cable remembered thinking. It's too bad. But I want to go home too, and the way it is now both of us won't be able to. They're going to cry and that's too bad. But everything's too bad. For one brief moment he had thought, remembering it clearly now: Get down, you fool! Stop showing yourself!

Then someone was shaking his foot. He looked back at a bearded face. The face nodded twice. Cable touched the trooper next to him and whispered, indicating the Yankee picket, "Take him."

The man next to him pressed his cheek to his Enfield, aiming, but taking too long, trying to hold the barrel steady, his whole body shivering convulsively from the long, rain-drenched hours. "Give me it," Cable whispered. He eased the long rifle out in front of him carefully and put the front sight just below the Indiana man's face. You shouldn't have looked at him through the glasses, he thought, and pulled the trigger and the picket across the stream was no more. They were up and moving after that. Not until evening did Cable have time to remember the man who had waited helplessly, unknowingly, to be killed. . . .

The way Vern Kidston is now, Cable thought.

There was no difference between the two men, he told himself. Vern was a Yankee; there was no question about that. The only difference, if you wanted to count it, was that Vern didn't have a blue coat or a flat forage cap with the bugle Infantry insignia pinned to the front of it.

What if the 51st Indiana man had had a different kind of hat on but you still knew what he was and what he was doing there?

You would have shot him.

So the uniform doesn't mean anything.

It's what the man believes in and what he's doing to

95

you. What if Vern were here and you were down there, the places just switched?

The thumb of Cable's right hand flicked the trigger guard down and up, levering a cartridge into the breech. The thumb eased back the hammer. Cable brought his face close to the carbine and sighted down the short barrel with both eyes open, placing the front sight squarely on the small figure in the trees. Like the others, Cable thought. It would be quick and clean, and it would be over.

If you don't miss.

Cable raised his head slightly. No, he could take him from here. With the first one he would at least knock Vern down, he was sure of that. Then he could finish him. But if Vern reached cover?

Hit his horse. Then Vern wouldn't be going anywhere and he could take his time. He wondered then if he should have brought extra loading tubes with him. There were four of them in his saddle bag. Each loading tube, which you inserted through the stock of the Spencer, held seven thick .56-56 cartridges. The Spencer was loaded now, but after seven shots—if it took that many—he would have to use the Walker.

Vern Kidston moved out of line. Cable looked up, then down again and the Spencer followed Vern to his horse, hardly rising as Vern took up the reins and stepped into the saddle.

Now, Cable thought.

But he waited.

He watched Vern come out of the trees, still on the far side of the river, and head north, the same way Lorraine had gone. Going home probably. Either by way of the horse trail or by following the long curving meadow all the way around. But why weren't they together? It was strange that Vern would let her ride home alone at this time of day. In less than an hour it would be full dark. Cable doubted that she knew the country that well.

Another thing. Where had they been? Why would they stand there talking for a while, then ride off separately?

Instantly Cable thought: You're letting him go!

He shifted the Spencer, putting the front sight on

Vern again. He held the carbine firmly, his finger crooked on the trigger and the tip of the barrel inching along with the slow-moving target. The distance between them lengthened.

You've got ten seconds, Cable thought. After that he wouldn't be sure of hitting Vern. His arms and shoulders tightened and for one shaded second his finger almost squeezed the trigger.

Then it was over. He let his body relax and eased the hammer down on the open breech.

No, you could have a hundred years and you wouldn't do it that way. There's a difference, isn't there? And you're sure of it now. You feel it, even if you can't define it.

Cable rose stiffly, watching Vern for another few moments, then trudged slowly back up through the pines.

Mounted again, he felt a deep weariness and he sat heavily in the saddle, closing his eyes time and again, letting the sorrel follow the path at a slow-walking pace. His body ached from the long all-day ride; but it was the experience of just a few minutes ago that had left the drained, drawn feeling in his mind. One thing he was sure of now, beyond any doubt. He couldn't kill Vern Kidston the way Janroe wanted it done. He couldn't kill Vern or Duane this way regardless of how logical or necessary the strange-acting, sly-talking man with one arm made it sound.

Knowing this, being sure of it now, was something. But it changed little else. The first move would still be Vern's. Cable would go home, not hurrying to an empty house, and he would hold on to his patience until he had either outwaited or outfought Vern once and for all.

He descended the slope behind the house, dismounted at the barn and led the sorrel inside. Within a few minutes he appeared again. Carrying the Spencer and the field glasses he walked across the yard, letting his gaze move out to the willows now dull gray and motionless against the fading sky. When he looked at the house he stopped abruptly. Lamplight showed in the open doorway.

His left hand, with the strap of the field glasses across the palm, took the Spencer. His right hand dropped to the Walker Colt and held it as he approached the house, passed through the semidarkness of the ramada and stepped into the doorway.

He stood rigid, seeing the strewn bedcovers, the slashed mattress, the soot filming the table and the caved-in stove chimney on the floor; seeing the scattered, broken ruin and Lorraine Kidston standing in the middle of it. She turned from the stove, sweeping aside fragments of china with her foot, and smiled at Cable. "I've been waiting for you."

Chapter Five

Cable said nothing, his eyes going to the shattered china still on the cupboard shelves, then to the stove again and to the battered chimney flue lying on the floor.

So Vern or Duane, or both of them, had become tired of waiting. Now they were doing something and this was a warning. Fix the house, Cable thought, then another time when you're away they tear it apart again. How much of that could you take? Do you run out of patience right now or later sometime?

He could release his anger and kick at the broken dishes or yell at Lorraine, threaten her, threaten her father and Vern. But what good would it do? That was undoubtedly their intention—to rile him, to make him start something. And once you did what the other man wanted you to, once you walked into his plan, you were finished.

Lorraine was watching him. "When the wife is away, the house just seems to go to ruin, doesn't it?"

He looked at her. "What do they expect me to do now?"

"I'm sure I don't know."

"Or care," Cable said.

"Well, I'm sorry; but there's nothing I can do about it, is there?"

"Did both of them have a hand in this?"

"I doubt if either of them did. They've been home all day."

"I just saw Vern."

"Alone?"

"You were with him."

99

"Do I have to explain what we were doing?"

"It doesn't matter."

"Vern and I went for a ride after supper. When we reached the meadow he said he wanted to look at his horses. I told him to go ahead, I was going home."

Cable said nothing.

"Well?" Lorraine looked at him inquiringly.

"All right. Then what?"

"Then I left him."

"And came to see what he did to the house."

Lorraine smiled, shaking her head. "Guess again."

"Some other time."

She caught the note of weariness in his tone. For a moment she said nothing, watching him stand the carbine next to the window and then move slowly to the table and place the field glasses there. "Did you see my horse outside?" she asked.

Cable glanced at her. "I didn't notice."

"No horse," Lorraine said lightly. "That's why I'm here." She watched Cable gather the blanket and comforter and pile them on the slashed mattress.

"I was going up the path behind your house, taking the short cut home, when something frightened my horse. It happened very suddenly; he lost his footing and started to slide back and that's when I fell off." Lorraine touched her hair lightly and frowned. "I hit my head."

Cable was looking at her again, sensing that she wasn't telling the truth. "Then what happened?"

"Then he ran off. I could hear him way up in the trees, but I couldn't very well chase after him, could I?"

"So you came to the house."

"Of course."

"You want me to look for your horse?"

"He's probably still running."

Cable paused. He was certain she was here for a reason and he was feeling his way along to find out what it was. "I've only got one horse here."

"I know," Lorraine said.

"You want me to ride you home?"

"The way my head hurts I don't know if I could stand it."

"Just for an hour? That's all it would take."

She was staring at Cable, not smiling now, holding him with the calm, knowing impudence of her gaze.

"We could wait until morning."

He almost knew she was going to say it; still, the shock, the surprise, was in hearing the words out loud. Cable's expression did not change. "What would your father say about that?"

"What could he say? I don't have a choice. I'm stranded."

Cable said nothing.

"Or I could tell him I spent the night outside." Lorraine smiled again. "Lost."

"You're serious, aren't you?"

"What do you think?"

"If you're ready, I'll saddle the horse."

"I told you, I couldn't bear the ride."

"You told me a lot of things."

The knowing, confident expression was in her eyes again. "I think you're afraid of me. Or afraid of yourself."

"Being alone with you?"

Lorraine nodded. "But I haven't decided which it is. The only thing I'm sure of is you don't know what to do. You can't take me home by force; and you can't throw me out. So?"

Momentarily, in his mind, he saw Lorraine at home sitting with Vern and her father evening after evening, looking up from her book and wanting to do something, anything, to break the monotony but having no choice but to sit there. Until she planned this, or somehow stumbled into it. Perhaps that was all there was to her being here. It was her idea of excitement, something to do; not part of a plan that involved Vern or Duane.

So, Cable thought, the hell with it. He was too tired to argue. Tired and hungry and her mind was made up, he could see that. He moved to the door of the next room, glanced in and saw that the two single beds had not been touched, then looked at Lorraine again.

"Take your pick."

She moved close to him in the doorway to look into the room. "It doesn't matter."

"Whichever one you want." He walked away from her and for the next few minutes concentrated on shaping

101

and straightening the stove flue. He was able to put it up again, temporarily, but his hands and face were smudged with soot when he'd finished.

Lorraine waited until he started a fire in the stove, then told him to go outside and wash; she'd fix something to eat. Cable hesitated, doubting her ability at the stove; but finally he went out—washed up at the river, scrubbing his hands with sand and scooping the cool water into his face. He felt better being alone outside and he took his time at the river, then went to the barn and looked in at the sorrel again before returning to the house.

Coffee was on the fire; Cable smelled it as he came in. For a moment he watched Lorraine making pancakes in the iron frying pan and he thought: She wants you to be surprised. But he turned away from her and busied himself sweeping up the broken china. After that he turned the slashed mattress on the bed and spread the bedcovers over it. When it was time to sit down she served him the corn meal cakes in a pie plate and poured his coffee into a tin drinking cup. Lorraine sat down with him, watching him eat, waiting for him to say something; but Cable ate in silence.

"Well, what do you think?"

"Fine." He was finishing the last of his coffee.

"Surprised I know how to cook?"

"You're a woman, aren't you?" he answered, knowing she would react to it, but saying it anyway.

"Does that follow," Lorraine said peevishly. "Just because you're a woman all you're to be concerned with is cooking and keeping house?"

"I didn't say that."

"You're probably hopeless. You deserve to live out here with a wife and three kids."

"You make it sound like a sentence."

"You *are* hopeless."

"And tired," Cable said. He got up from the table, walked around to Lorraine's chair and pulled it out for her. "So are you."

She looked up at him. "Am I?" Her tone was mild now.

"Tired out from that long ride with Vern." He took Lorraine by the arm to the bedroom. "Have a good sleep and before you know it it'll be time to fix breakfast." He pushed her inside and closed the door before she could say a word.

Cable blew out the lamp, then walked to the open front door and stood looking out at the night, letting the stillness and the breeze that was coming off the meadow relax him. This was good. But it was a peace that lasted only as long as the night. Slowly Cable sat down in the doorway. Take advantage of the peace you can feel, he thought. Sleep was good, but it wasn't something you could enjoy each minute of and know you were enjoying it.

So he sat in the doorway, feeling the silence and the darkness about him, thinking of his wife and children, picturing them in bed in the rooms above the store; then picturing them here, seeing himself sitting with the children close to him and talking to them, answering their questions, being patient and answering the questions that were unrelated or imaginary along with the reasonable ones. Clare would ask the most questions and through her eyes that were wide with concentration he could almost see her picturing his answers. It was like the times she would relate a dream she had had and he would try to imagine how she saw it with her child's eyes and with her child's mind. While he was talking to Clare, Davis would become restless and jump on his back, Davis with enough energy for all of them and wanting to fight or be chased or swim in the river. Sandy, lying against him, listening to them contentedly with his thumb in his mouth, would scowl and yell at Davis to stop it. Then he would quiet them and they would talk about other things until Martha called.

And after the children were in bed they would sit here on the steps, watching the willows turn to silent black shapes against the sky, hearing the night sounds in the pines and far out on the meadow. They would talk in low murmurs, feeling the familiar nearness of one another. They talked about the children and the house and about things they had done and about things they would do someday; but not talking about the future, because if they accomplished or acquired nothing more than what they had, it would be enough and they would be satisfied; perhaps as happy as anyone, any family, could expect to be.

If you can hold on to what you have, Cable thought. Right now you would settle just for that and not hope for anything more.

He was certain that the Kidstons had damaged the house, as a warning. Maybe not Vern. It seemed more like something Duane would do. But regardless of who did it, the effect was the same.

He heard the sound behind him, the bedroom door opening and closing. He turned, starting to push himself up, but Lorraine was already over him. Her hand went to his shoulder and she sank down beside him.

"I thought you were tired."

"I'm going to bed in a minute," Cable said. He saw that Lorraine was wearing one of Martha's flannel nightgowns. He had felt it as she brushed against him to sit down.

"What were you thinking about?"

"A lot of things at once, I suppose."

"Vern and Duane . . . the happiness boys?"

He looked at her. "I'd like to know what you're doing here."

"I explained all that."

"You didn't any more get thrown than I did."

Lorraine smiled. "But I had to tell you something."

"Did Vern send you?"

"Don't be silly."

"Then what are you doing here?"

"Keeping you company."

"I guess you are."

Lorraine moved, rising to her knees and turning to him. Her hands went to his shoulders, then to his face caressingly as she kissed him.

"You're not very responsive, are you?" She pressed close to him, kissing him again. "In fact you're rather cold. I'm surprised."

"You've got the wrong one, that's all."

"Oh, come now—"

"Or else the wrong time and place."

"Would you like to go somewhere else?"

Quietly, Cable said, "Lorraine, you're probably the pleasantest temptation I've ever had—but I've got enough things living in my mind the way it is."

Close to him her head moved slowly from side to side. "The only halfway decent looking man within fifty miles and he has to have a conscience." She felt his hands circle her waist and when they lingered, holding her, she said, "I'll give you one more chance."

But now he pushed her away and rose, lifting her with him. "I don't think this would do either of us any good."

In the darkness her eyes remained on him, but it was some time before she said, "I suppose your wife is very fortunate. But I doubt if I'd want to be married to you. I can't help feeling there's such a thing as being too good."

The next morning Cable cleaned the main room and fixed the stove flue more securely. Later on, he decided, he would ride to Denaman's Store. He would buy plates and cups, probably tin ones if Janroe had any at all; and he would stay as long as he could with Martha and the children.

Cable was outside when the two Kidston riders came by. He saw them crossing the river, approaching cautiously, and he walked out from the ramada, the Walker on his leg. He waited then as the two riders came across the yard toward him. A vague memory of having seen them before made Cable study their faces closely. No, he was certain he didn't know them. Still—

The two riders looked somewhat alike, yet the features of one appeared more coarse and his coloring was freckled and lighter than the other man. It was as if both of their faces—both narrow and heavy boned—had been copied from the same model, but one had been formed less skillfully than the other. Both wore full mustaches and the darker of the two men showed a trace of heavy beard, at least a week's growth.

"If you're looking for Lorraine," Cable said, "you've found her."

The two riders were watching Cable, but now their eyes rose past him as Lorraine appeared.

She seemed a little surprised. "How did you know I was here?"

"Your daddy's got everybody looking everywhere,"

the dark man said. There was no trace of concern in his voice.

"Is he worried?"

"About out of his mind."

"I can just see him." Lorraine stepped down from the doorway and walked out to them. "You two will have to ride double," she said, looking up. Neither of the men made a move to dismount. Lorraine moved toward the dark rider's chestnut gelding. "This one." Still the man hesitated and Lorraine added, "If you don't mind."

"Where's yours?"

"I have no idea," Lorraine answered.

The dark rider's gaze moved to Cable. "Maybe we ought to use his then."

Lorraine's face showed sudden interest. "If he'll let you."

"He will."

"We can't do it while the girl's here," the other man said then. "Duane wouldn't have any part of that."

"I suppose we got time," the dark one grunted.

"All we want," the other rider said.

The dark one swung down. Not bothering to help Lorraine, he walked past her, raised his hand to the other rider and was pulled up behind him. He looked down at Cable again.

"Long as we got time."

They rode out, past the house to the horse trail that climbed the slope. In the saddle now, straddling it with her skirt draped low on both sides, Lorraine waited long enough to say, "That was Austin and Wynn Dodd."

Cable frowned. "I don't know them."

Lorraine smiled pleasantly. "You knew their brother. Joe Bob."

She rode off toward the slope, following the Dodd brothers. Before passing into the pines behind the house, Lorraine looked back and waved.

There were times when Janroe could feel his missing hand; times when he swore he had moved his fingers. He would be about to pick something up with his left hand, then catch himself in time. A moment before this Janroe had absently raised his missing arm to lean on the door

106

frame. He fell against the timber with his full weight on the stump, and now he stood rubbing it, feeling a dull pain in the arm that wasn't there.

Luz Acaso appeared, coming from the back of the building. She was riding her dun-colored mare, sitting the saddle as a man would, her bare legs showing almost to her knees. Two of the Cable children, Clare and Davis, were following behind her as she crossed the yard toward the river.

Janroe stepped out to the loading platform.

"Luz!" The dun mare side-stepped as the girl reined in and looked back at him.

"Come over here."

She held the horse, standing almost forty feet from the platform. "I can hear you," she said.

"Maybe I don't want to shout."

"Then you come over here!"

Don't ruffle her, Janroe thought. Something was bothering her. He had first noticed it as she served him his breakfast. She seldom spoke unless he said something to her first, so her silence this morning wasn't unusual. Still, he had sensed a change in her. Her face was somber, without expression, yet he could feel a new tension between them. Even when she served him she avoided his eyes and seemed to reach out to place the coffee and food before him, as if afraid to come too close to him.

That was it. As if she was guarding something in her mind. As if she was so conscious of what she was thinking, she felt that if he looked in her eyes or even came too close to her, he would see it.

But while he was eating he would feel her eyes on him, watching him carefully, intently; although when he looked up from his plate she would be turning away or picking something up from the stove.

Now she was riding down to Hidalgo. Tonight there would be a gun shipment and Luz would lead it to the store, making sure the way was clear. Janroe said, "You're leaving a little early, aren't you?"

"I want to have time to see my brother."

"About what?"

"Nothing."

"You seem anxious enough over nothing."

107

"I want to see him, that's all." She waited a moment longer, watching Janroe, but when he said no more she flicked the reins and moved on across the yard. Janroe watched her pass into the willows and even after she was out of sight he continued to stare at the trees. What was it about her—was she more confident? More sure of herself since the Cables had come home. Afraid when she was alone with him, still somewhat more confident.

He noticed the Cable children then. Clare and Davis were still in the front yard, standing close to each other now and looking up at him on the platform.

"I told you once to play in the back," Janroe called out. "I'm not going to tell you again. I'll get a stick next time, you understand?"

Clare stood rigid. Davis nodded with a small jerk of his head and reached for Clare's arm. They turned to go.

"Wait a minute." Janroe looked down at them sternly. "Where's your father? Is he still here?"

"Upstairs," the boy said.

"All right." Janroe waved them away and they ran, glancing back at him as they rounded the corner of the building.

What do you have to do to a man like that? Janroe thought. A man that finds his house wrecked and comes moping in to buy tin plates and sit with his wife. Cable had arrived about mid-morning and had been here ever since.

Janroe stood for some time holding the stump of his arm, rubbing it gently. He was looking above the willows now, to the hillside beyond the full roundness of the tree tops. But it was moments before he realized a file of riders had come down out of the pines and was descending the slope.

Perhaps because his hand still held the stump, or because he had jarred it and imagined the pain still present; because of this and then abruptly seeing the riders on the hillside and for the moment not caring who they were—his mind went back to another time, another place. . . .

There had been riders then on a hillside; directly across the cornfield and not more than eight hundred yards away, a line of riders appearing along the crest of the hill, then stopping and dismounting. He had seen that

they were unhitching the horses from artillery pieces—
three of them—and rolling the guns into position.

He had waited then, studying the position through his
field glasses for at least ten minutes, or perhaps a quarter
of an hour; so by the time he brought his men out of the
pines, screaming at them, shooting one and seeing the
other soldier who had been afraid suddenly run by him,
the field pieces were ready and loaded and waiting for
him.

Janroe himself was no more than a hundred yards
out from the woods when the first shell exploded. The
blast was loud in his ears and almost knocked him down;
but he kept moving, seeing two, then three, men come
stumbling, crawling out of the smoke and dust that seemed
to hang motionless in the air. One of the men fell face-
down and didn't move. As he watched, a second and third
shell exploded and he saw one of the crawling men lifted
from the ground and thrown on his back. Close around
him men were flattening themselves on the ground and
covering their heads.

But the ones in front of him were still moving, and
with the next explosion Janroe was running again. He saw
the man who had been afraid a few moments before, running, breathing heavily, his head back as if he was looking
up at the three artillery pieces. Janroe was close to the
man, almost about to run past him and yell back at him to
keep coming, and then the man was no more.

It was as if time suddenly stopped, for Janroe saw the
man, or part of him, blown into the air and he could
remember this clearly, the fraction of a moment caught
and indelibly recorded in his mind. And it was the same
sudden, ground-lifting, sound-smashing burst of smoke and
iron that slammed Janroe senseless and cleanly severed his
left arm. . . .

For some time the line of riders was out of sight, low
on the slope now and beyond the bank of willow trees.
Janroe waited, watching, judging where they would cross
the river and appear out of the tree shadows. They would
be Kidston riders, Janroe was certain of that. He wondered if he should call Cable. No, wait, Janroe decided.
Act natural and just let things happen.

There were six of them. Janroe recognized Duane

Kidston at once: Duane sitting a tall bay horse with one hand on his thigh, a riding quirt hanging from his wrist and his elbow extended rigidly. Duane wearing the stiff-crowned Kossuth hat squarely on his head, the brim pinned up on one side with the regimental insignia. Duane playing soldier, Janroe thought contemptuously. Pretending that he's a man.

Have your fun, Major, Janroe thought then, not taking his eyes from Duane. Have all the fun you can. Your time's about run out.

Briefly he noted the five men with Duane: Bill Dancey, the solemn, bearded one close to Duane's right; then the two Dodd brothers, Austin and Wynn. They had been here only once before but Janroe remembered them well, the brothers of one of the men Cable had killed. Austin and Wynn Dodd, one light, the other dark, but both with angular, expressionless faces. Janroe remembered their eyes; they watched you coldly, impersonally, as if you were a thing that couldn't look back at them.

Janroe was not sure if he had ever seen the two other riders before. He watched these two veer off midway across the yard and circle to the back of the store.

Moments later the two Cable children, Clare and Davis, came running around from the back yard. Then, seeing the four riders approaching the platform, they stopped and stood watching, their eyes wide with curiosity.

"Where is he?" Duane asked.

"Inside." Janroe moved nearer the edge of the platform.

"Get him out."

"What for?"

"That's my business."

"You want to kill him?"

"Duane's got things to say to him," Dancey said then.

Janroe's eyes moved to the bearded man. "I wouldn't want to think I fetched him to be killed."

"We're not going to kill him," Dancey said.

"That would be an awful thing to have on your conscience," Janroe said. "Calling a man to be killed in front of his children."

Dancey shook his head. "You've got my word."

"And with his wife here too," Janroe said. "I couldn't ever face her again."

"Mr. Janroe," Duane said, "if you don't get him out here, you can be assured we will."

Janroe looked past the men to the Cable children. His eyes settled on Clare.

"Honey, go tell your daddy there's some men here to see him."

Clare hesitated, but Davis pushed her and she ran up the steps to the platform, holding close to the wall as she ran by Janroe and into the store.

"Fine youngsters," Janroe said pleasantly. "He's got three of them." Duane wasn't listening. He glanced at Dancey. Then Dancey and the Dodd brothers dismounted and came up the steps to the loading platform. Duane remained in his saddle.

"Where is he?" Dancey asked.

"Upstairs a few minutes ago."

"He mention what happened last night?"

"Not a word." Janroe's tone indicated only mild interest. "What did?"

"About Lorraine—"

"No!" Janroe's face showed surprise, then an eager curiosity. "What happened?"

But Dancey's gaze moved beyond him. Janroe turned. He heard the steps on the plank floor then Cable, wearing his Walker Colt, was standing in the doorway. Janroe saw Martha and the little girl a few steps behind him.

"Take off that gun," Dancey said.

Cable looked from Dancey to the Dodd brothers—to Austin, the dark one, who was a step nearer than Wynn—then back to Dancey.

"What's this about?"

"Take it off," Dancey said again. "You're covered front and back."

Cable heard the quick steps behind him. He seemed about to turn, but he hesitated. The two riders who had circled the adobe had entered by the back door and had waited for Cable behind the counter. Now one of them pulled the Walker from its holster. Feeling it, Cable glanced over his shoulder. He saw the second man standing close to Martha.

As Cable turned back to Dancey, Austin Dodd moved. He stepped in bringing his balled left hand up from his side. Before Cable saw it coming the fist slammed into his face. He fell against the door frame, went to his hands and knees with his head down and close to the platform boards. Austin Dodd followed through. His right hand came up with his Colt, his thumb already hooking back the hammer.

"Hold on!" Dancey stepped in front of him. "We didn't come here for that." He looked out at Duane Kidston angrily. "You'd have let him, wouldn't you?"

"Austin has his own reason," Duane said. "Stopping him wouldn't be any of my business."

"We didn't come here to satisfy Austin," Dancey grunted.

Duane stared at the bearded foreman. "I'm beginning to wonder why I brought you."

"You wouldn't've if Vern had been around. You said you wanted to talk to this man. That's all."

"I'm going to."

"But you'd have let Austin kill him."

"It wasn't your brother Cable shot down," Duane said flatly. "That's the difference."

"He took him in a fair fight."

"We're not even sure of that. All we know is Joe Bob and Royce came home face-down over their saddles," Duane said. "And it wasn't your daughter he—"

Duane stopped. His eyes went to Cable who was still on one knee, but watching Duane now.

"Get him up."

Dancey moved aside. He said, "Go ahead," and stepped back to the edge of the platform near Janroe. The Dodd brothers pulled Cable to his feet. They planted themselves close to him, each holding an arm with both hands. Cable stood quietly, making no attempt to free himself. Behind them, Dancey could see Martha and the little girl in the square of light formed by the doorway. Martha seemed calm, Dancey judged. But you couldn't tell about women. The little girl was afraid. And the little boy—Dancey's gaze moved to the steps where Davis was squatting now—he's wondering what they're doing to his pa and he wouldn't believe it if somebody told him.

Duane called, "Jimmie!" and one of the men who'd covered Cable from behind came out to the platform. Duane raised his reins, then dropped them and the man came down; but not until he'd picked up the reins did Duane dismount. He stepped down stiffly, straightened his coat, then walked around to the steps and up to the platform, past Davis without even glancing at him though he touched him with his riding quirt, in a gesture of brushing the boy aside.

His full attention was on Cable now. Duane stepped squarely in front of him, close to him, and stood for some moments in silence, his legs apart and his hands fisted on his hips. But before he spoke his hands dropped to his sides.

"I should let Austin kill you," Duane said. "But I can't do it. God knows everyone here would be better off for it, but I can't pass final judgment on a mortal man, not even after he's done what you did."

"What did I do?" Cable asked, not with surprise or indignation, but calmly, wondering what had suddenly brought Duane here.

"Offended innocence," Duane said. "You'd better keep your mouth shut. I've taken all of you I can stomach."

"I asked a civil question."

Duane's quirt came up and lashed across Cable's face. "And I said shut up!" He stepped back as Cable twisted to free himself. Wynn Dodd stumbled to one knee and Cable almost broke away, but Austin forced Cable's right arm behind his back and jerked up on it.

"I'll break it!"

Cable stopped struggling. He let his breath out slowly and his body seemed to sag. His eyes went to Davis still watching him from the steps, then away from the boy quickly, back to Duane.

"Do you have to do this in front of my children?"

Duane stepped close to him again. "How much respect did you show my daughter?"

"What did Lorraine say I did?"

"She didn't have to say anything. She was all night at your place."

Janroe, near the edge of the platform, looked at Martha, but her eyes were on her husband. He noticed Duane's gaze move to her then.

"You hear that Mrs. Cable? Your husband and my daughter."

"He told me about it," Martha said quietly.

"He told you, did he." Duane's mouth barely moved. "Did he tell you how he dragged Lorraine into that hut?" He turned on Cable and in the motion slashed the quirt across his face. "Did he tell you how he kept her there all night?" The quirt came back across Cable's face. "How he threatened her and forced his will on her?" He swung on Cable again and again, hacking at Cable's cheeks and forehead with the rawhide. Cable's eyes were squeezed closed and he would turn his head with each stinging blow. But he was off balance, leaning forward awkwardly, and he was unable to turn his body with Austin holding his arm twisted behind him. Duane struck him eight times before his arm dropped heavily to his side.

"Did he tell you all that, Mrs. Cable?"

"He told me everything that happened."

"His version."

"If you've finished, Mr. Kidston, may I take my husband inside?"

Duane stared at Martha, his face tight as he held back the temper ready to flare out at her calm, quiet manner.

He said then, "If you want him, take him. Take him anywhere you like, but not back to your house. You're finished here, and I believe you're intelligent enough to realize it. If you think this is unjust, that's too bad; your husband is lucky to be alive. I'll tell you frankly, if it wasn't for your children he would be dead now."

Bill Dancey watched Martha, waiting for her to speak again; but Martha said nothing, her hand on the little girl close to her side. Dancey walked across the platform. Going down the steps he patted Davis's shoulder, but the boy pulled away from him. Dancey mounted, then looked up at Duane.

"You've said it. What're you waiting for?"

Duane still faced Martha. He ignored Dancey, and said, "This evening my men leave for the horse pastures. They'll be gone one week. If you haven't cleared out by the time they return, we will take your husband out and hang him. That's my last warning, Mrs. Cable."

Duane turned and marched stiffly down the steps to his horse. The Dodd brothers followed, almost reluctantly, both of them looking back at Cable as they mounted and rode out after Duane.

Janroe came away from the edge of the platform and studied Cable's face closely. "Duane laid it on you, didn't he?"

Cable said nothing. He felt Martha standing next to him now, but he continued to watch the riders. When they had finally crossed the river and started up the slope, he looked at Janroe.

"That one Duane called Jimmie—what did he do with my gun? Did you see?"

Janroe stepped to the edge of the platform again and looked down. "He dropped it right there."

"Get it for me."

Janroe seemed to smile. "I'd be glad to."

Cable felt Martha's hand on his arm. He looked at her, at her soft, clear expression, at her eyes that seemed moist, though he wasn't sure if she was crying.

She said, "Cabe, come inside now."

He followed her through the store, through the main room to the kitchen, then sat down while Martha went to the sink. She dipped water from a bucket into a kettle, and put the kettle on the stove to heat.

Clare and Davis appeared in the doorway, staring at their father until Martha noticed them and told them to go outside and play.

Cable looked up. "No, let them stay," he said. He motioned to the children. They came in hesitantly, as if this man with the red welts across his face was someone neither of them had ever seen before. But when he smiled and held out his arms, both of them ran to him and pressed against his chest. He kissed Clare on the cheek, then Davis. The boy's arms went around his neck and clung to him and Cable felt the knot in his stomach slowly begin to relax.

Martha poured the warm water into a basin. She carried it to the table, then leaned close to her husband and began bathing the swollen red marks that crossed both of his cheeks, his nose and his forehead. A bruise colored his cheekbone where Austin Dodd had hit him.

Cable's eyes raised. "Where's Sandy?"

"Still taking his nap."

"I'm glad he didn't see it."

Martha said nothing. She moved the two children aside to give herself more room, then pressed the wet cloth gently to Cable's forehead.

"The second time they've seen me beaten," Cable said. "Beaten up twice in front of my children—standing there turning the other cheek while a man rawhides my face."

Martha raised his chin with her hand. "Cabe, you don't have to prove yourself to them. You're their father."

"Something they don't have anything to say about."

"They'd love you under any circumstance, you know that."

"Then it's a question of proving myself to me."

Martha shook her head. "It isn't a matter of principle, a question of whether or not you're a man. This is something that affects the whole family. We want to go home and live in peace. Clare and Davis and even Sandy, we want what is rightfully ours, but we don't want it without you."

"Then you want to leave here," Cable said.

"I didn't say that. If we run away, we lose. But if we have to bury you, we lose even more."

"Martha, I don't have a choice."

She leaned close to him with her hands on the arms of the chair. "Cabe, don't go after them just because of what Duane did."

"You know it's more than that."

"You were beaten up in front of the children. Right now that's all you can think about."

"Sooner or later this will be settled with guns," Cable said. "It might as well be now."

"It doesn't have to be that way," Martha said urgently. "If we wait, if we can put it off— Cabe, something could happen that would solve everything!"

"Like what?"

She hesitated. "I'm not sure."

"Martha, I'm awful tired of waiting."

She looked at him intently. "You could go to Fort Buchanan. Put it up to the authorities."

"You know who they'd side with."

"But we're not sure. Cabe, at least it's worth trying."

From the doorway Janroe said, "I've got the only way to solve your problem." He extended Cable's Walker Colt, holding it in the open palm of his hand. "Right here."

Martha turned, looking at him coldly. "That would solve nothing."

"All right," Janroe said. "Go up to Buchanan. Tell the Yankees you're a Rebel soldier come home to find a gang of Yankee horse-breakers using your land and threatening to hang you." Janroe moved into the kitchen. "You know what they'd do? Supply the rope."

Martha motioned the two children to the back door. She held it open for them, then, closing it behind them, looked at Janroe again.

"Mr. Janroe, I don't think this concerns you."

"Ask your husband whether it concerns me or not." He stopped in front of Cable and handed him the revolver. "Right?"

Cable said nothing. He took the Walker and looked at it idly, holding it in both hands.

Janroe watched him. "You're going back to your place?"

Cable nodded.

"That's the right direction," Janroe said mildly. His eyes remained on Cable's lowered head. "Did you hear what Duane said about his men going off this evening? They'll go over to some pastures Vern's got way north and west of here and start working the herds home. Duane said they'd be gone a week." Janroe shook his head. "They'll be gone longer than that. And just Duane and maybe Vern will be home, just the two of them."

Cable looked up. "You told me that once before."

Janroe nodded. "And Duane confirmed it." His voice lowered. "It would be easy for a man like you. Ride in there and take both of them."

Martha came away from the door. "You're asking my husband to commit murder!"

Janroe glared at her. "Like any soldier murders."

"This isn't war—he isn't a soldier now!"

"We've been all through that," Janroe said. "Whether it bothers his conscience or not, your husband doesn't have a choice. He's got to kill them before they kill him."

That evening, as soon as it was dark, Janroe slipped under the platform and let himself into the locked storeroom. He measured three strides to the crates of Enfield rifles stacked against the back wall, then stood in the darkness, wondering if there would be room for the wagon-load of rifles due to arrive later that night. The rifles that were here should have been picked up days ago.

You can worry about it, Janroe thought, or you can forget it and ask Luz when she comes. She should be here within two hours. Perhaps they told her in Hidalgo why the rifles had not been picked up. Perhaps not. Either way, there was something more immediate to think about. Something raw and galling, because it was fresh in his mind and seemed to have happened only moments before though it had been this afternoon, hours ago.

He had almost convinced Cable. No, not almost or maybe. He had convinced him. He had handed the man his gun and told him to kill the Kidstons or be killed himself, and Cable had seen the pure reality of this. If he had left at that moment, he would have gone straight to the Kidston place. Janroe was sure of it.

But Martha had interfered. She talked to her husband, soothing the welts on his face with a damp cloth while she soothed his anger with the calm, controlled tone of her voice. And finally Cable had nodded and agreed not to do anything that day. He would go home and watch the house—that much he had to do—but he would not carry the fight to the Kidstons; at least not while he felt the way he did. He agreed to this grudgingly, wearily, part by part, while Martha reasoned in that quiet, firm, insisting, never-varying tone.

Perhaps if he went out to see Cable now? No, the guns were coming and he would have to be here. In the morning then; though by that time the sting would be gone from the welts on Cable's face and that solid patience would have settled in him again.

He had *convinced* Cable—that was the absolute truth

of it—until the woman had started in with her moral, monotonous reasoning—

Janroe straightened. He stood listening, hearing the faint sound of a horse approaching. The hoof beats grew louder, but not closer, and when the sound stopped, he knew the horse had reached the back of the store.

Luz? No, it was too early for her. He left the storeroom, carefully, quietly padlocking the door, came out into the open and took his time mounting to the platform and passing through the darkened store. He saw Martha first, standing in the kitchen, then Luz, and saw the girl's eyes raise to his as he moved toward them.

"You're early."

"They're not coming," Luz said.

"What do you mean they're not coming?"

"Not any more."

"All right," Janroe said. "Tell me what you know."

"The war's over."

She said it simply, in the same tone, and for a moment Janroe only stared at her.

"What are you talking about?"

"It's true," Martha said. "They told her as soon as she reached Hidalgo."

He looked at Martha then, seeing her face no longer composed but for the first time flushed and alive and with a smile that was warm and genuine and seemed to include even him, simply because he was here to share the news with them.

He turned to Luz again. "Who told you?"

"Everyone knows it. They told me to come back and tell you."

"But how do they know? How can they be sure?"

"They know, that's all."

"Listen, wars don't just end like that."

"How do they end?" Martha asked, not smiling now.

"There's some warning—days, weeks before, that it's going to end."

"You know how news travels out here," Martha said.

"No"—Janroe shook his head—"we would have heard something. It's a false alarm, or a Yankee trick. It's something else because a war just doesn't end like that."

"We're telling you that the war is over," Martha said.

119

"Whether you believe it or not it ended five days ago, the day we came home."

"And they're just finding out now?" Janroe shook his head again. "Uh-unh, you don't sell me any of that."

"Would they have lied to Luz?"

"I don't even know what they told her! How do I know she even went there?"

Martha was staring at him. "You don't want to believe it."

"What am I supposed to believe—everything this girl comes in and tells me?"

"Luz"—Martha glanced at the girl—"can I take your horse?"

Janroe saw Luz nodding and he said anxiously, "What for?"

"To tell my husband," Martha answered, looking at him again.

"You think you should?" Janroe asked. It was moving too fast again, rushing at him again, not giving him time to think, and already it was the next step, telling her husband. They would not just stand and talk about it and see how ridiculous the news was; they would bring Cable into it, and if he argued about the sense of her going she would go all the quicker.

"I mean riding out alone at night," Janroe said. He shook his head. "I couldn't see you doing that."

"I think my husband should know," Martha began.

"I believe that," Janroe said. The words were coming easier now. "But I think I better be the one to go tell him."

Martha hesitated. Before she could say anything, Janroe had turned and was gone. She looked at Luz, but neither of them spoke, hearing Janroe just in the next room.

When he came into the kitchen again he was wearing a hat and a coat, the armless sleeve flat and ending abruptly in the pocket, but bulging somewhat with the shape of a shoulder holster beneath the coat.

"You *will* see him?" Martha said. "I mean make sure he finds out?"

"Don't worry about it."

"And you promise to tell him everything?"

"I won't be long." Janroe went out the back door and mounted Luz Acaso's dun mare.

He crossed the river and hurried the dun up the slope to the horse trail, following it north, almost blindly in the night darkness of the trees, brushing branches in his haste and kicking the dun. He moved along the ridge, though with no intention of visiting Cable.

He knew only that there was no time for Cable now. He could admit that to himself without admitting the other, that the war was over. Certainly it could be at the very edge of the end. This could be the last day. It might very well be the last day. All right, it *was* the last day and now there was no time for Cable. The war was not over yet, he told himself, but there was time to do only one thing now.

Four, raging, uninterrupted years of war did not end with two women standing in a kitchen and saying that it was over. You would expect that of women. It was typical. A woman would tell you anything. Lies became truth to them because they felt justified in using any means at hand to hold life to a sweet-smelling, creeping pace; to make this a woman's existence with no room for war or fighting or so many of the things that men did and liked to do and only really proved themselves as men when they were doing them.

If he had not entered the kitchen he wouldn't have heard anything. A man couldn't wait and plan for eight months and know what he had to do, and then see it all canceled by walking into a kitchen. That couldn't be.

So the two women had lied and it was stupid to think about it. And even if it was not a matter of their lying, then it was something else, something equally untrue; and whether the something was a lie from the women or a trick or an untruth from another source was beside the point.

He was hurrying, as if to keep up with time, so that not another moment of it would go by before he reached the Kidston place. But even after half admitting this was impossible he told himself that right now was part of a whole time, not a time before or a time after something. It was a time which started the day he came to live at the store and would end the day he saw the Kidstons dead. So this was part of the time of war. But almost as he thought this, it became more than that. Now, right now, was the whole of the war, the everything of a war that would not end until the Kidstons were dead.

It took him less than an hour altogether. By the time he left the horse trail he had cleared his mind of everything but the Kidstons. Winding, moving more slowly through the sandstone country, he was able to calm himself and think about what he would do after, what he would do about Cable, what he would tell Martha and Luz. Martha . . .

By the time he reached the edge of the timber stand bordering the Kidston place, looking across the open area to the house and outbuildings, he was composed and ready. He was Edward Janroe who happened to be riding by, say, on his way to Fort Buchanan. He was a man they had seen at least once a week for the past eight months. He was the one-armed man who owned the store now and didn't say much. He was nothing to be afraid of or even wonder about. Which was exactly the way Janroe wanted it.

Chapter Six

J anroe came out of the trees, letting the dun mare move at its own pace toward the house. He was aware of someone on the veranda, certain that it was Duane when he saw the pinpoint glow of a cigar.

There was no hurry now. Janroe's eyes rose from the veranda to the lighted second-story window, then beyond the corner of the house, past the corral where a dull square of light showed the open door of the bunkhouse. There were no sounds from that end of the yard, none from the big adobe that was pale gray and solid looking in the darkness. The cigar glowed again and now Janroe was close.

"Good evening, Major."

Duane leaned forward, the wicker chair squeaking. "Who is it?"

"Edward Janroe." Now, almost at the veranda, Janroe brought the dun to a halt. He saw Duane rise and come close to the railing, touching it with his stomach.

"I didn't mean to startle you," Janroe said.

"You didn't startle me." There was indignation in Duane's tone.

"I meant you sitting here by yourself. . . . Is Vern about?"

"No, he's up at his pastures. You wanted to see him?"

"I'd like to have. But I guess you can't have everything."

"What?"

"Where's Vern, out on the horse drive?"

"Getting it started. He's been gone all day."

123

"You alone?"

"My daughter's in the house."

"And somebody's out in the bunkhouse."

Duane seemed annoyed, but he said, "A couple of the men."

"I thought everybody went out on the drives," Janroe said.

"We always keep one man here."

"You said a couple of men were there."

As if remembering something, Duane's frown of annoyance vanished. "The second man rode in a while ago to tell us the news. I've been sitting here ever since thinking about it." Duane paused solemnly. "Mr. Janroe, the war is over. Lee surrendered the Army of Northern Virginia to General Grant on April ninth."

"Is that a fact?" Janroe said.

"I have been thinking of a place called Chancellorsville," Duane said gravely. "I have been thinking of the men I knew who died there: men I campaigned with who gave their lives that this final victory might be accomplished."

"A touching moment," Janroe said.

Duane's eyes rose. "If you had served, you would know the feeling."

"I served."

"Oh? I didn't know that. In the Union army?"

"With Kirby Smith."

"Oh. . . . You lost your arm . . . were wounded in battle?"

"During the fight at Richmond, Kentucky."

"Is that right? I was in Cincinnati at the time. If I hadn't been on my way to Washington, I would have answered General Nelson's call for volunteers."

"That would have been something," Janroe said, sitting easily and looking down at Duane, "if we'd fought against each other."

Duane nodded gravely. "More terrible things than that have actually happened. Brother fighting brother, friend against friend. The wounds of our minds as well as those of our bodies will have to be healed now if we are to live together in peace." Duane added, for effect, "The war is over."

"You're not just telling me that?" Janroe said.

"What?"

"That the war's over."

"Of course it is. The word came direct from Fort Buchanan. They learned about it this afternoon. Their rider ran into Vern, and Vern sent a man here to tell us. Vern realized I would want to know immediately."

"I haven't been told," Janroe said. "Not officially, and your telling me doesn't count."

Duane was frowning, squinting up at Janroe in the darkness with his cigar poised a few inches from his face. "How could you learn more officially than this? The message came from Fort Buchanan, a military establishment."

"You learned it from your side," Janroe said. "I haven't been told officially from mine."

"Man, you've been out of the war for at least a year! Do you expect them to tell personally every veteran who served?"

"I haven't been out of it." Janroe paused, studying Duane's reaction. "I'm still fighting, just like you've been with your saddle-tramp cavalry, like your brother's been doing supplying Yankee remounts."

Duane was squinting again. "You've been at your store every day. I'm almost sure of it."

"Look under the store," Janroe said. "That's where we keep the Enfields."

"British rifles?"

"Brought in through Mexico, then shipped east."

"I don't believe it." Duane shook his head. "All this time you've been moving contraband arms through the store?"

"About two thousand rifles since I started."

"Well," Duane said, officially now, "if you have any there now, I advise you to turn them over to the people at Fort Buchanan. I presume Confederate officers will be allowed to keep their horses and sidearms, but rifles are another matter."

Janroe shook his head slowly. "I'm not turning anything over."

"You'd rather face arrest?"

"They can't take me if they don't know about the guns."

"Mr. Janroe, if you don't turn them in, don't you think I would be obligated to tell them?"

"I suppose you would."

"Then why did you tell me about them?"

"So you would know how we stand. You see, you can be obligated all you want, but you won't be able to do anything about it."

Duane clamped the cigar in the corner of his mouth. "You've got the nerve to ride in here and threaten me?"

"I guess I do." Janroe was relaxed; he sat with his shoulders hunched loosely and his hand in his lap.

"You're telling me that I won't go to Buchanan?" Duane's voice rose. "Listen, I'll take my saddle-tramp cavalry, as you call it, and drag those guns out myself, and I'll march you right up to the fort with them if I feel like it. So don't go threatening me, mister; I don't take any of it."

Janroe watched him calmly. "It's too bad you didn't volunteer that time you said. That would have made this better. No, it would have made it perfect—if you had been in command of that Yankee artillery company. They were up on a ridge and we had to cross a cornfield that was trampled down and wide open to get at them. They began firing as soon as we started across. Almost right away I was hit and my arm was torn clean from my body."

"I think we've discussed this enough for one evening," Duane said stiffly.

"What if you had given that order to fire?" Janroe said. "Do you see how much better it would make this?" He shook his head then. "But that would be too much to ask; like having Vern here too. Both of you here, and no one else around."

"I would advise you to go home," Duane said, "and seriously consider what I told you. I don't make idle threats."

"I don't either, Major." Janroe's hand rose to the open front of his coat. He drew the Colt from his shoulder holster and cocked it as he trained it on Duane. "Though I don't suppose you'd call this a threat. This is past the threatening stage, isn't it?"

"You don't frighten me," Duane said. He remembered something Vern had told Cable that day at Cable's house, rephrasing it now because he was not sure of the exact words.

"There is a big difference between holding a gun and using it. If you're bluffing, Mr. Janroe, trying to frighten me, I advise you to give it up and go home."

"I'm not bluffing."

"Then you're out of your mind."

"Major, I don't think you realize what's happening."

"I realize I'm talking to a man who hasn't complete control of his faculties."

"That's meant to be an insult, nothing else," Janroe said. "If you believed it, you'd be scared out of your wits."

Duane hesitated. He watched Janroe closely, in silence; the hand holding the cigar had dropped to his side. "You wouldn't dare use that gun," he said finally.

"It's the reason I came."

"But you have no reason to kill me!"

"Call it duty, Major. Call it anything you like." Janroe put the front sight squarely on Duane's chest. "Do you want to run or stand there? Make up your mind."

"But the war's over—don't you realize that!"

Janroe pulled the trigger. In the heavy report he watched Duane clutch the railing, holding himself up, and Janroe fired again, seeing Duane's body jerk with the impact of the bullet before sliding, falling to the porch.

"It's over now," Janroe said.

He reined and kicked the dun to a gallop as he crossed the yard. Behind him he heard a window rise and a woman's voice, but the sounds seemed to end abruptly as the darkness of the trees closed in on him.

Now back to the store. There was no reason to run. He would tell the women that Cable was not at home, that he'd looked for him, but with no luck. Tomorrow he would ride out again, telling the women he would try again to locate Cable.

But he would take his time, giving Vern time to learn about his brother's death; giving him time to convince himself that it was Cable who'd killed Duane; giving him time, then, to go after Cable. No, there was no need to run.

It had been a satisfying time. The best since the days near Opelousas when he'd killed the Yankee prisoners.

Bill Dancey had spent the night in a line shack seven miles north of the Kidston place. The day before, after the incident at Denaman's, after watching Duane demonstrate his authority with a rawhide quirt, after riding back to the Kidston place with Duane and the Dodd brothers and not speaking a word to them all the way, Dancey had decided it was time for a talk with Vern.

But Vern was still away. Since that morning he'd been visting the grazes, instructing his riders to begin driving the horses to the home range. Vern could be gone all night, Dancey knew, and that was why he went out after him. What he had to say wouldn't wait.

By late evening, after he had roamed the west and north pastures, but always an hour or more behind Vern, Dancey decided to bed down in the line shack. It was deserted now, which suited him fine. It was good to get away from the others once in a while, to sit peacefully or lie in your blanket with quiet all around and be able to hear yourself think. It gave him a chance to review the things he wanted to tell Vern.

With the first trace of morning light he was in the saddle again; and it was at the next pasture that he learned about Duane. There were five men here, still at the breakfast fire. They told him that Vern had been here; but a rider came during the night with news about Duane —one before that with word about the war being over; it had sure as hell been an eventful night—and Vern had left at once, taking only the two Dodd brothers with him.

By six o'clock Dancey was back at the Kidston place. He crossed the yard to the corral, unsaddled and turned his horse into the enclosure before going on to the house.

Austin and Wynn Dodd were sitting on the steps: Wynn sitting low, leaning forward and looking down between his legs; Austin sitting back with his elbows resting on the top step, Austin with his head up, his stained, curled-brim hat straight over his eyes. Both men wore holstered revolvers, the butt of Wynn's jutting out sharply from his hip because of the way he was sitting. Austin, Dancey noticed then, was wearing two revolvers, two Colts that looked like the pair Joe Bob had owned.

Dancey stopped in front of them. "Vern's inside?"

Wynn looked up. Austin nodded.

"He told you to wait for him?"

"Right here." Wynn leaned back saying it, propping his elbows on the step behind him.

"If that's all right with you, Bill," Austin said dryly.

Dancey moved through them to the porch. He opened the screen then stood there, seeing Vern and Lorraine at the stove fireplace across the room. Dancey waited until Vern saw him before moving toward them.

"I've been looking for you." Vern said it bluntly, and the tone stirred the anger Dancey had held under control since yesterday afternoon.

He wanted to snap back at Vern and if it led to his quitting, that was all right. But now Duane was dead and before he argued with Vern he would have to say he was sorry about Duane. And Lorraine was here. Her presence bothered him too. She didn't appear to have been crying, but stood staring at the dead fire; probably not even thinking about her father, more likely wondering what was going to happen to her. She seemed less sure of herself now; though Dancey realized he could be imagining this.

He looked at Vern. "Your brother's dead?" And when Vern nodded Dancey said, "I'm sorry about it. Where is he now?"

"Upstairs. We'll bury him this afternoon."

"All right." Dancey's eyes moved to Lorraine. "What about his girl?"

"I think she'll be going back home," Vern said. "This brought her up pretty short. She might have even grown up in one day."

"It could do that," Dancey said. "When was it, last night?"

Vern nodded. "He rode in while Duane was on the porch. Lorraine was upstairs. She heard the two shots and looked out her window in time to see him riding off."

"Who's he?"

"Who do you think?"

"Did she see him clearly?"

"She didn't have to."

"It's best to be sure."

"All right, Bill, if it's not Cable, who would it be?"

"I know. It's probably him; but you have to be sure."

"I'm sure as I'll ever be."

Vern moved past him and Dancey followed out to the porch. The two Dodd brothers were standing now, watching Vern.

"There'll be just the four of us," Vern told them. He waited until they moved off, then seemed to relax somewhat, leaning against a support post and staring out across the yard. He said to Dancey behind him, "They'll bring you a fresh horse."

"I can get my own," Dancey said.

"I guess you can, but they'll bring it anyway."

"Now we go visit Cable—is that it?"

"You don't have to come."

"Then I sure as hell don't think I will."

Vern turned suddenly from the post, but hesitated then. "Bill, do you realize the man's killed three people now, one of them my brother?"

"Are you telling me you're going after Cable because you and Duane were so close?"

"Be careful, Bill."

"What would you have done if two men came to your house at night—two men like Royce and Joe Bob? What would you have done if somebody busted your house—"

"I had no part of that; you know it."

"Duane said yesterday he didn't either." Dancey paused. "Maybe Lorraine just made it up." The tone of his voice probed for an answer.

But Vern said only, "Who did it isn't my concern."

"All right," Dancey said. "How would you see it if somebody had taken a rawhide quirt to your face while two others held your arms?"

"I don't have to see it! The man killed my brother, do you understand that?"

"You've got something to say for your stand." Dancey saw the anger etched deeply in Vern's eyes, hardening the solemn, narrow-boned look of his face. "But what are you going to do about it?"

"Take him up to Fort Buchanan."

"You better go in shooting."

"If that's the way it has to be."

"It's the only way you'll beat him," Dancey said. "And even then he'll fight harder than you will. He's got his family and his land at stake."

Vern shook his head. "This has gone beyond arguing over land."

"You've got three hundred horses up in the high pastures," Dancey said. "When you bring them down they're going to have water. That's the point of all the talk. Nothing else. You've got horses relying on you. He's got people. Now who do you think's going to swing the hardest?"

Vern watched the Dodd brothers coming, leading the horses, then looked at Dancey again. "I'll give him a chance to go up to Fort Buchanan peacefully. If he refuses, that's up to him."

Dancey shook his head. "You'll have to kill him."

"I said it's up to him."

"Maybe you'd hold back." Dancey watched the Dodd brothers approaching. "But they wouldn't. They'd give up a month's pay to draw on him." Dancey hesitated, and when Vern said nothing he added, "You've got yourself talked into something you don't even believe in."

"Listen," Vern said tightly, "I've said it, if he won't come peacefully, we'll shoot him out."

"But you're hoping he'll listen to you."

"I don't care now."

"He won't," Dancey said. "And not one person in his family would. I saw that yesterday. I saw it in his wife and kids, his little boy standing there watching his daddy get rawhided and the kid not even flinching or crying or looking the other way. The man's family is with him, Vern. They're part of him. That's why when you fight him you'll think you're fighting five men, not just one."

"There'll be four of us, Bill," Vern said. "So that almost evens it." He started down the steps.

"Three," Dancey said. "I'll drive your horses. I will this time. But I won't take part in what you're doing."

Vern was looking up at Dancey again, studying him, but he said only, "All right, Bill," as if he had started to say something else but changed his mind. He moved to his horse and mounted, not looking at Dancey now, and led the two Dodd brothers out of the yard.

They'll kill Cable, Dancey thought, watching them go. But they'll pay for it, and not all three of them will come back.

Cable was in the barn when Luz Acaso came.

Earlier, while he was fixing something to eat and had gone to the river for a bucket of water, he saw Kidston's mares and foals out on the meadow. He had planned to run them two days ago, but Manuel had come and he had forgotten about the horses until now. So after breakfast he mounted the sorrel and again chased the herd up the curving sweep of the valley to Kidston land.

He was back, less than an hour later, and leading the sorrel into the barn, when he heard the horse coming down through the pines from the ridge trail. He waited. Then, seeing Luz Acaso appear out of the trees and round the adobe to the front yard, Cable came out of the barn. But in the same moment he stepped back inside again.

Two riders were coming along the bank of the river on the meadow side. Then, as they jumped their horses down the bank, starting across the river, Cable turned quickly to the sorrel. He drew the Spencer from the saddle, skirted the rectangle of light on the barn floor and edged close to the open doorway.

From this angle, looking past the corner of the house, he saw Luz Acaso first, Luz standing close to her dun horse now, staring out across the yard. Then beyond her, he saw the two riders come out of the willows. One was Vern Kidston. Cable recognized him right away. The other was one of the Dodd brothers, and Cable was almost sure it was the one named Austin.

But why didn't they sneak up?

No, they couldn't have seen him. He had stayed close to the trees coming back from running the horses and he had been in the yard, after that, only a moment. Watching them now, he was thinking: If they wanted to kill you they would have sneaked up.

Unless—he thought—there were more than just the

two of them. Vern could be drawing him out. Wanting him to show his position, if he was here.

So wait a minute. Just watch them.

But there was Luz to think of.

His gaze returned to the girl. She was facing Vern, still standing by her horse; but now, as Cable watched, she dropped the reins and moved toward the two riders, walking unhurriedly and with barely a trace of movement beneath the white length of her skirt. Vern Kidston came off his saddle as she approached them.

Cable heard him ask, "Where is he?" the words faint and barely carrying to him. Luz spoke. There was no sound but he saw her shrug and gesture with her hands. Then Kidston spoke again, a sound reaching Cable but without meaning, and he saw Luz shake her head.

For several minutes they stood close to each other, Luz looking up at Kidston and now and again making small gestures with her hands, until, abruptly, Vern took her by the arm. Luz resisted, trying to pull away, but his grip held firmly. Vern walked her to the dun, helped her onto the saddle and the moment she was seated, slapped the horse sharply across the rump. He watched her until she passed into the aspen stand a dozen yards beyond the adobe, then motioned to Austin Dodd.

Austin caught up the reins of Vern's horse and came on. Cable watched him, wondering where the other Dodd brother was. Wynn. He had seen them only twice, but still he could not picture one without the other. Perhaps Wynn was close by. Perhaps that was part of these two standing out in the open.

Austin reached Vern and handed him the reins. Cable waited. Would Vern mount and ride out? If he did, it would be over. Over for this time, Cable thought. Then he would wait for the next time—then the next, and the time after that. Unless you do something now, Cable thought.

Tell him, and make it plain—

No, Cable knew that to make his stand clear and unmistakably plain, without the hint of a doubt, he would have to start shooting right now, right this second. And that was something he couldn't do.

He did not see this in his mind during the moments of waiting. He didn't argue it with himself; but the doubt, the conscience, the whatever it was that made him hesitate and be unsure of himself, was part of him and it held him from killing Vern Kidston now just as it had prevented him from pulling the trigger once before.

Briefly, he did think: You can be too honest with yourself and lose everything. He hesitated because this was a simple principle, a matter of almost black or white, and whatever shades of gray appeared, whatever doubts he might have, were still not strong enough to allow him to shoot a man in cold blood.

Though there was more to it than that. A simple principle, but not a simpler matter. Not something as brutally, honestly simple as war. He couldn't shoot Vern in cold blood. But if he *could* . . . If the urge to end this was stronger than anything else, would his shooting Vern end it? Would he be sure of getting Austin, too? Then Wynn and Dancey and Duane . . . and how many more were there?

It wasn't good to think. That was the trouble, thinking about it and seeing it as black and white and good and bad and war or not war. Wouldn't it be good if they could go back six days and start over and not have the Kidstons here or Janroe, not have anything that has happened happen, not even in a dream?

No, it was not merely a question of not being able to shoot Vern in cold blood. It never was just that. It was being afraid, too, of what would happen to his family. To him, and then to his family.

If they would fight, he thought. If they would hurry the hell up and fight, you could fight back and there would be nothing else but that to think about and there wouldn't even be time to think about that.

He saw Vern Kidston draw his revolver. He saw Austin Dodd dismounting, pulling a Sharps rifle from his saddle boot. Both men walked toward the adobe and within a few strides, from this angle, watching them from the barn and looking past the front corner of the house, they passed from Cable's view.

They'll wreck it for good this time, Cable thought.

If you let them.

He felt the tenseness inside of him, but he was not squeezing the Spencer and his legs felt all right. Stepping out from the barn, he glanced toward the back of the adobe. The clearing between the pine slope and the house was empty. Then he was running across the yard, watching the front now, until he reached the windowless side wall of the house. He edged along to the front, cocked the Spencer and stepped around.

Vern and Austin Dodd were coming out of the front door, under the ramada now, Vern with his hands empty, his Colt holstered again, Austin Dodd holding the Sharps in one hand, the barrel angled down but his finger through the trigger guard. Both men saw Cable at the same time, and both were held motionless by the same moment of indecision.

Cable saw it. He stopped, ready to fire if either man moved a finger, waiting now, leaving the decision with them and almost hoping to see the barrel of the Sharps come up.

"Make up your mind," Cable said, even though he felt the moment was past. He moved toward them, along the log section of the house, until less than a dozen strides separated him from the two men.

"You came to wreck it a second time?"

"I came to talk," Vern said flatly. "That first."

"With your gun in your hand."

"So there wouldn't be an argument."

"Well, you've got one now."

Vern's gaze dropped to the carbine. "You better put that down."

"When you get off my land."

"If you want a fight," Vern said, with the same sullen tone, "one of us will kill you. If you want to come along peacefully, I give you my word we won't shoot."

"Come where?"

"To Fort Buchanan."

Cable shook his head. "I've got no reason to go there."

Vern stared at him, his full mustache accentuating the firm line of his mouth. "I'm not leaving before you do," he said. "Either shoot your gun off or let go of it."

Almost at once Cable had sensed the change in Vern Kidston. Four days ago he had stood covering Vern with a gun and Vern had calmly told him that he would outwait him. But now something had changed Vern. Cable could hear it in the flat, grim tone of the man's voice. He could see it on Vern's face: an inflexible determination to have his way now. There would be no reasoning with Vern, no putting it off. Cable was sure of that. Just as he knew he himself would not be budged from this place by anything less persuasive than a bullet.

Still, momentarily, he couldn't help wondering what had brought about the change in Vern, and he said, "So you've lost your patience."

"You visited Duane last night," Vern said. "We're returning the call."

"I never left this house last night."

"Like you don't know anything about it."

"Well, you tell me what I did. So I'll know."

"In case you didn't wait to make sure," Vern said, "I'll tell you this. Duane's dead. Either one of the bullets would have killed him."

Cable stared at Vern, almost letting the barrel of the Spencer drop and then holding it more firmly. He could not picture Duane dead and he wondered if this was a trick. But if Vern was making it up, what would it accomplish? No, Duane was dead. That was a fact. That was the reason Vern was here. And somebody had killed him.

Janroe.

Janroe, tired of waiting. Janroe, carrying the war, his own private version of the war, to Duane. It could be Janroe. It could very well be and probably was without any doubt Janroe.

But he couldn't tell Vern that. Because to convince Vern it was Janroe he'd have to explain about the man, about the guns, and that would involve Luz and Manuel. And then Vern would go to the store and Martha and the children were there now, and they'd seen enough . . . too much. Besides, this thing between him and Vern still had to be settled, no matter what Janroe had done.

Cable said, "I didn't kill your brother. If I had sneaked up to kill anybody, if I'd carried it that far, it would have been to put a sight on you."

"You're the only man who had reason to do it," Vern said.

"That might seem to be true," Cable answered. "But I

didn't. Like you're the only one who had reason to wreck my house. Did you do it?"

"I never touched your place."

"So there you are," Cable said. "Maybe we're both lying. Then again, maybe neither of us is."

"You're not talking your way out of it," Vern said flatly.

"I don't have to." Cable raised the carbine slightly. "I'm holding the gun."

"And once you pull the trigger, Austin will put a hole through you."

"If he's alive," Cable said, centering his attention on Austin Dodd who was still holding the Sharps in one hand, the tip of the barrel almost touching the ground. The man seemed even more sure of himself than Kidston. He studied Cable calmly, with an intent, thoughtful expression half closing his eyes.

Like you don't have a gun in your hand, Cable thought, watching him. He's not worried by it because he knows what he's doing. So you go for Austin first if you go at all.

In his mind he practice-swung the Spencer on Austin, aiming to hit him just above his crossed gun belts. When a man is stomach-shot he relaxes and there is no reflex action jerking his trigger, no wild dead-man-firing. Then he pictured swinging the carbine lower and farther to the left. Austin might drop and roll away and it would be a wing shot, firing and letting the man dive into it. No, it wouldn't be like that, but that's the way it would seem. He thought then: That's enough of that. If you have to think when it's happening, you'll be too late.

The silence lengthened before Austin Dodd spoke.

"He talks, but he's scared to do anything."

Kidston said nothing.

Austin Dodd's eyes still held calmly, curiously on Cable. "I've got him thought out but for one thing. Where'd he buy the nerve to kill Joe Bob?"

"Ask him," Kidston said.

"He'll say he killed him fair." Carefully, Austin raised his left hand and pulled on the curled brim of his hat, loosening it on his head and replacing it squarely.

"Maybe," he said then, "we ought to just walk up and take the gun away from him."

Cable watched him. A moment before, as Austin adjusted his hat, he was sure the man's eyes had raised to look past him. And just before that Austin had started talking. Not a word from him until now.

To make sure you keep looking at him, Cable thought. He felt his stomach tighten as he pictured a man behind him, a man at the corner of the house or coming carefully from the direction of the barn with his gun drawn. Austin was staring at him again. Then—there it was—Vern Kidston's gaze flicked out past him. Vern looked at Cable then, quickly, saw his intent stare, and let his gaze wander aimlessly toward the willows.

Now you're sure, Cable thought, wanting to turn and fire and run and not stop running until he was alone and there was quiet all about him with the only sounds in the distance.

But he made himself stand and not move, his mind coldly eliminating the things that could not happen: like whoever it was being able to sneak up close to him without being heard; or suddenly shooting Vern and Austin Dodd standing directly in front of him, in the line of fire.

So, it would be timed. The moment they moved, the second they were out of the way, the man behind him would fire. It came to that in Cable's mind because there was no other way it could be.

And it would come soon.

Watch Austin and go the way he goes.

It would be coming now.

But don't think and listen to yourself.

You'll hear it. God, you'll hear it all right.

You'll even see it. You'll see Austin—

And Cable was moving—spinning to the outside, pushing himself out of the line of fire and throwing the carbine to his shoulder even before Austin Dodd and Kidston hit the ground. With the sound of the single shot still in the air, he was putting the carbine on Wynn Dodd, thirty feet away and in the open, standing, holding his Colt at arm's length.

Cable fired. *Too soon!* He saw Wynn swing the Colt on him as he levered the Spencer, brought it almost to his shoulder and fired again. Wynn was turned, thrown off balance by the impact of the bullet and his Colt was pointing at the willows when it went off. Still, he held it, trying to bring it in line again; but now Cable was running toward him, levering the trigger guard, half raising the carbine and firing again. Wynn's free hand went to his side and he stumbled, almost going down. From ten feet, with Wynn's Colt swinging on him and seeming almost in his face, Cable shot him again, being sure of this one, knowing Wynn would go down; and now levering, turning, snapping a shot at Austin Dodd and missing as the man came to one knee with the Sharps almost to his shoulder.

Austin and Vern had held their fire because of Wynn, but now both of them opened up. Cable's snap shot threw Austin off and he fired quickly, too wide. From the ramada, Kidston fired twice. Before he could squeeze the trigger again Cable was past the corner of the adobe, beyond their view, and within ten strides safely through the open doorway of the barn.

He brought the sorrel out of its stall, thonging the Spencer to the saddle horn, then mounted and drew the Walker.

Now time it, Cable thought.

He knew what Kidston and Austin would do, which was the obvious thing, the first thought to occur to them; and they would respond to it because they would have to act fast to keep up with him or ahead of him and not let him slip away.

Only one man could watch the barn from the corner of the house. The second man would have to expose himself, or else drop back to the willows, to the protection of the cutbank and move along it until he was opposite the barn, directly out from it and little more than a hundred feet away. If that happened he would be pinned down in the barn until he was picked off, burned out or eventually drawn out by a need as starkly simple as a cup of water. If he waited, time would be on their side to be used against him.

So he would move out and he would do it now while they were still realizing what had to be done, while they were still scrambling to seal off his escape. He knew this almost instinctively after two and a half years with Bedford Forrest. You weren't fooled by false security. You didn't wait, giving the other man time to think. You carried the fight, on your own terms and on your own ground.

Now it was a matter of timing. Move fast, but move at the right time.

The sorrel was lined up with the doorway now, though still well back in the barn. From here Cable could see the corner of the adobe. As he watched he saw a man's shoulder, then part of his head and the dull glint of a Colt barrel in the sunlight. Almost at the same time he heard the horse somewhere off beyond the adobe—the other man running for the cutbank.

Cable's eyes clung to the corner of the house.

Now move him back, he thought, raising the Walker and putting the front sight on the edge of the house. He fired once. The man—Cable was sure it was Kidston—drew back out of sight. At that moment Cable moved, abruptly spurring the sorrel. He was suddenly in the sunlight and reining hard to the right, the Walker still covering the corner; and as Kidston appeared, coming suddenly into the open, Cable fired. He had to twist his body then, his arm extended straight back over the sorrel's rump. He fired again, almost at the same time as Kidston did, but both of their shots were hurried. Then he was reining again, swerving the sorrel to the left, passing behind the adobe just as Kidston fired his second shot.

Even as he entered the horse trail up into the pines, Cable saw the way to throw the fight back at them, to swing on them again while they were off guard in the true hell-raising, hit-and-run style of Forrest; and he left the trail, coming back down through the trees. Then he was in the open again behind the adobe, but now cutting to the right and circling the side of the adobe away from the barn. A moment later he broke past the front of the house.

Twenty feet away Kidston was mounting, looking directly at Cable over the pommel of his saddle. He saw Vern trying to bring up his Colt. He saw Vern's face clearly beyond the barrel of his own revolver; he was pulling the trigger when Vern's horse threw its head into the line of fire. Cable reined the sorrel hard to the right then, seeing Vern's horse stumble and go down with Vern falling and rolling clear.

He caught a glimpse of Austin Dodd already mounted and coming up over the cutbank, but that was all. There was one shot left in the Walker and now Cable was spurring, running the sorrel through the light- and dark-streaked aspen stand, then cutting to the left, reaching the willows, brushing through them and feeling the thick, heavy branches behind him, covering him as he splashed across the river and climbed out onto the meadow.

Get distance on Austin, that was the thing to do now. Get time to reload, and at the same time look like you're running. Now he would lead Austin, let Austin think he was chasing him, and perhaps he would become careless.

Austin fired the Sharps as he came out of the willows to the edge of the river, but he hurried the shot and now Cable was almost two hundred yards ahead of him, holding the sorrel to a steady run.

Cable was calm now. Even though he was sure only in a general way what he would do. Somehow, he would stop Austin Dodd just as he had stopped Vern.

But was Vern stopped? For how long? He could be coming too. He would find Wynn's horse, which might or might not take time; but he would come.

So it wasn't over, or even halfway over. It was just starting. He would have to be careful and keep his eyes open and stop Austin—Austin first. Now it was a matter of leading him on until he found the place he wanted to fight him. He was applying what he had learned well with Bedford Forrest. How to kill and keep from being killed. Though not killing with an urge to kill, not killing Austin Dodd because he was Austin Dodd. Though you could probably even justify that, Cable thought.

He would start up the far side of the meadow and be in the trees while Austin was still in the open. Then Austin would slow up and that would give him time to reload. That would be the way to do it, he thought, lifting his gaze to the piñon trees and the open slope that rose above them.

Yet it was in the same momentary space of time, with the heavy, solid report, with the unmistakable smacking sound of the bullet, that Cable's plan dissolved. The sorrel went down, shot through a hind leg, and Cable was suddenly on the ground. He rolled over, looking back in time to see Austin Dodd mounting again.

The man had reloaded on the run, got down for one last-chance long-shot with the Sharps at two hundred stretching to three hundred yards. And you weren't watching!

Cable started for the sorrel—on the ground with its hind legs kicking in spasms. The Spencer was still thonged to the saddle. The cartridge tubes and loads for the Walker were in the saddle bags. But he knew at once that it was too late to get them. If he delayed, he'd be pinned down behind the sorrel. In Cable's mind it was not a matter of choice. Not with a slope of thick piñon less than forty yards away.

He ran for it, crouched, sprinting, not looking back but hearing the hoof beats gaining on him; then the high, whining report of a Colt.

Before Austin could fire again, Cable was through the fringe of yellow-blossomed mesquite and into the piñons. From here he watched Austin rein in at the sorrel and dismount. Cable was moving at once, higher up on the slope, a dozen yards or more, before he looked back at Austin again.

The gunman was squatting by the sorrel going through the one accessible saddle bag. But now he rose, holding the Spencer down-pointed in one hand, stepped back and shot the sorrel through the head. He threw the carbine aside, looking up at the piñon slope.

"Cable!" Austin shouted the name. He paused while his eyes scanned the dark foliage. "Cable, I'm coming for you!"

Cable watched him, a small figure forty or fifty yards below him and out in the open, now coming toward the trees.

He's sure of himself, Cable thought. Because he's been counting shots and he knows it as well as you do. Cable pulled the Walker and checked it to be sure.

One bullet remained in the revolver. Extra loads, powder and percussion caps were all out in the saddle bag.

Luz kept the dun mare at a steady run, her bare knees pressed tightly to the saddle, holding it and aching with the strain of jabbing her heels into the dun's flanks.

She realized she should have taken the horse trail. It was shorter. But Vern Kidston had sent her off abruptly, and in the moment her only thought had been to keep going, to run for help as fast as the dun would move. And now she was following the curving five-mile sweep of the meadow, already beyond the paths that led up to the horse trail from Cable's land.

They would find Cable in the barn. . . She had seen him go in as she approached. And if he showed himself, they would kill him. Even if he didn't, he was trapped. She pictured Vern and the other man firing in at him, not showing themselves and taking their time. But if they waited, having trapped him, she might have time also—time to bring help.

If her brother was home. She had thought of no one else, picturing him mounting and rushing back to Cable's aid. He would *have* to be home. God, make him be home, she thought, closing her eyes and thinking hard so God would hear her; he said he would come today, so all You have to do is make sure of it. Not a miracle. Just make him be home.

And if he's not? Then Mr. Janroe.

No! She rejected the thought, shaking her head violently. God is just. He couldn't offer something that's evil to do something that's good.

Yet in the good act, saving Cable, Vern Kidston could be wounded or killed. And there would be nothing good in that.

She closed her eyes as tightly as she could to see this clearly, but it remained confused, the good and the evil overlapping and not clearly defined or facing one another as it should be. Because the wrong ones are fighting, she thought.

But why couldn't they see this? Vern Kidston and Paul Cable should be together, she thought, because they are the same kind of man; though perhaps Paul is more gentle. He has a woman and has learned to be gentle.

But Vern could have a woman. And he could also learn to be gentle. She knew this, feeling it and knowing it from the first time she saw him; feeling it like a warm robe around her body the time he kissed her, which had been almost a year ago and just before Janroe came. Then feeling it again, standing close to him and seeing it in his eyes as they faced each other in front of Cable's house.

She had told him Cable was not at home and he said, then they would wait for him. I will wait with you, Luz said. But Vern shook his head saying, go on home to Janroe. She told him then, without having to stop to think .of words, what she thought of Edward Janroe, what kind of a half-man half-animal, what kind of a *nagual* he was. And she could see that Vern believed her when she said she despised Janroe.

She had pleaded with him then to put his guns aside and talk to Cable, to end it between them honestly as two men should. She had thought of the war being over, saying: see, they ended after seeing how senseless it was that so many men should die. End your war, too, she had said.

But he had taken her arm and half dragged her to the dun mare and told her to go. Because now it was this business with Cable and not a time for gentleness. He did not say this, but Luz could feel it. Just as she knew now why he had stopped seeing her after Janroe's coming.

Because Vern Kidston was proud and would rather stay away and clench his fists than risk discovering her living with or in love with Edward Janroe. That meant only one thing. Vern Kidston loved her. He did before and he did now.

But don't think of it now, she thought. Don't think of anything. Just do what you have to do. She told herself that this was beyond her understanding. For how could there be room for love and hate in the same moment? How could good be opposed to good? And how can you be happier than you have been and more afraid than you have ever been, both at the same time?

Within a few minutes she was in sight of the store with the dark sweep of willows bunched close beyond. She kept her eyes on the adobe now and soon she was able to make out a figure on the platform. She prayed that it was Manuel.

But it was Janroe, standing rigidly and staring at her,

waiting for her as she crossed the yard and reined in the dun.

"Where've you been?"

She saw the anger in his face and in the tense way he held his body. But there was no time to be frightened; she wanted to tell him, she wanted to say all of it at once and make sure he understood.

"I went to the Cable place," she began, out of breath and almost gasping the words.

"I told you I was going there!" Janroe's voice whipped at her savagely, then lowered to the hoarse tone of talking through clenched teeth. "I told you to stay home, that I was going later—but you went anyway! I told you he wasn't there last night and I would see him this morning—but you went anyway!"

"Listen to me!" Luz screamed it, feeling a heat come over her face. "Vern Kidston is there—"

Janroe stared at her and slowly the tightness eased from his face. "Alone?"

"One man with him. Perhaps more."

"What happened?"

"Not anything yet. But something has happened to Vern and he wants to kill Cable. I know it!"

Janroe's chest rose and fell with his breathing, but he said calmly, "He probably just wants to talk to Cable."

"No—he was armed. Vern, and the one called Austin with two guns and a rifle on his saddle. . . . Listen, is my brother here?"

"Not yet."

"He said he was coming today."

"Probably later on."

She was looking at him intently now, trying to see something in him that she could trust, that she could believe. But there was no time even for this and she said, "Come with me. Now, before they kill him."

"Luz, Vern just wants to talk with him." Janroe was completely at ease now. "Vern's a patient man. Why would he change?"

"Then you won't come," Luz said.

"There's no need to. Come in the house and stop worrying about it."

She shook her head. "Then I'm going back."

145

"Luz, I said come in the house. It's none of your business what's going on between them."

She saw the anger in his face again and she raised the reins. Janroe came off the platform, reaching for the bridle, but the dun was already side-stepping, wheeling abruptly, and Janroe was knocked flat. Luz broke away and was across the yard before Janroe could push himself to his feet.

She held herself low in the saddle and kept the dun running with her heels and with her voice, making the horse strain forward and stretch its legs over the grass that seemed to sweep endlessly toward the curve of the valley.

She would do something, she told herself, because she had to do something. There was no one else. She wouldn't think of it being over. She would arrive before they found Cable and plead with Vern, not leaving this time even if he tried to force her. He would listen. Then Paul would come out and they would talk, and after a while the thing between them would be gone.

But only moments later she knew she was too late. Luz slowed the mare, rising in the saddle and pulling the reins with all her strength to bring the dun finally to a halt. She sat listening.

Now, in the distance, she heard it again: the flat, faraway sound of gunfire, and she knew they had found him and were trying to kill him.

Chapter Seven

Soon there would be two of them.

Cable could see the rider now—it would have to be Vern on Wynn's horse—already on this side of the river and coming across the meadow.

Below, closer to him, was Austin Dodd.

Cable waited until Austin came through the yellow mesquite patches at the edge of the piñon pines. As the man reached the trees, Cable began to fall back. He moved carefully up the slope, glancing behind him, not wanting to stumble and lose time, and not wanting to lose sight of Austin. He caught glimpses of the man moving cautiously up through the trees.

The slope was not steep here and the piñon seemed almost uniformly spaced, resembling an abandoned, wild-growing orchard. It was not a place to stand with one shot in his revolver and fight a man who had two Colt guns and all the time in the world.

Cable moved back until he reached the end of the trees. And now he stopped to study the open slope behind him. It was spotted with patches of brittlebush and cliff-rose, but nothing to use for cover; not the entire, gravelly, nearly one hundred feet of it that slanted steeply to the sky.

Perhaps he could make it; but not straight up. It was too steep. He would have to angle across the slope and Austin would have time to shoot at him. But it was worth trying and it would be better than staying here. He would have to forget about Austin—and about Vern, almost

147

across the meadow now—and concentrate on reaching the crest, not letting anything stop him.

He was in the open then, running diagonally across the rise, his boots digging hard into the crusted, crumbling sand. Almost at once he felt the knotted pain in his thighs, but he kept going, not looking back and trying not to picture Austin Dodd closing in on him; or Vern, at the foot of the slope now and taking out his rifle.

Cable cut through a patch of brittlebush, getting a better foothold then and running hard, but he came suddenly onto a spine of smooth rock—it humped no more than two feet above the ground—and here he slipped to his hands and knees. He tried to get up and stumbled again, then rolled over the side of the smooth rock surface before lunging to his feet. He was climbing again, less than twenty feet from the top when Austin's voice reached him.

"Cable!"

He stopped, catching his breath and letting it out slowly before coming around. He knew he would never make the crest. He was sure of it then, seeing Austin already well out of the piñon, to his left below him and less than sixty feet away. Austin's Colts were holstered, but his hands hung close to them. He came on slowly, his face calm and his eyes not straying from Cable.

"Pull anytime now," Austin said. He advanced up the slope, not looking at the ground but feeling his way along with each careful step.

"You want to. But you got only one shot." He was reaching the brittlebush now. "Count the other man's shots. That's something I learned a long time ago. Then when I saw your extra loads still out there with the horse I said to myself, 'I wouldn't want to be that boy. He don't have one chance between hell and breakfast.'"

Cable said nothing. He stood facing Austin Dodd, watching him move into the small field of orange-colored brittlebush. There Austin stopped.

"So when you pull," Austin said, "you have to make it good the one time." He seemed almost to be smiling. "That could tighten a man's nerves some."

Austin was ready, standing on his own ground. And to beat him with one shot, Cable knew, he would have to be more than fast. He would have to be dead-center accurate.

But he wouldn't have time to aim, time to be sure.

Unless Austin hesitated. Or was thrown off guard.

Cable's gaze dropped from the brittlebush to the smooth spine of rock where he had slipped. If he could draw Austin to that point. If he could jiggle him, startle him. If he could throw Austin off balance only for a moment, time enough to draw and aim and make one shot count. If he could do all that—

And Vern was into the piñon now.

No—one thing at a time.

Slowly then, Cable began to back away.

Austin shook his head, "You wouldn't come near making it."

Cable was still edging back, covering six, eight, almost ten feet before Austin started toward them again. Cable stopped. He watched Austin come out of the brittlebush, watched him reach the spine of rock and grope with one foot before stepping onto the smooth, rounded surface.

As Austin's foot inched forward again, Cable went to the side, dropping to one knee and bringing up the Walker in one abrupt motion.

Austin was with him, his right-hand Colt out and swinging on Cable; but the movement shifted his weight. His boots slipped on the smooth rock and even as he fired and fired again he was falling back, his free hand outstretched and clawing for balance.

Beyond the barrel of the Walker, Austin seemed momentarily suspended, his back arched and his gun hand high in the air. Cable's front sight held on his chest and in that moment, when he was sure and there was no doubt about it, Cable squeezed the trigger.

He was sliding down the gravel as Austin fell back into the brittlebush, reaching him then, knowing he was dead and concentrating on prying the revolver from the man's fingers. Cable took both of Austin's revolvers, both Colt Army .44s. He waited a moment, but there was no sign of Vern. He rose half crouched, expecting to hear Vern's shot, expecting to feel it, then ran for the piñon pines.

He went down beneath a tree, feeling the sand and grass patches warm and the thick branches close above him, and now he listened.

Vern would be close. In the time, he could have come all the way up through the trees. Perhaps not; but at any rate Vern would have seen him running across the open. Probably he was just not in position for a shot. But now Vern knew where he was; that much was certain.

So move, Cable thought.

He pushed up to one knee and waited, listening, then was running again, keeping low and dodging through the brushlike trees. Almost immediately a rifle report whined through the grove. Cable dropped, clawing then, changing his direction and moving down the slope. The firing began again, this time with the sound of a revolver somewhere between fifty and a hundred feet away from him. Cable kept going and the .44 sound hammered after him, five times, until he dropped into a shallow gully.

Cable rolled to his stomach, holstered one of the Colt's, and at once began crawling up the narrow wash, up toward the open slope. He moved quickly, using his knees and forearms, until he was almost to the edge of the trees, roughly thirty feet above the spot where he had entered the gully. He stopped then to listen.

There was no sound. Beyond the brush and rock shadows close in front of him, the slope glared with sunlight. He turned, looking back the way he had come, then removed his hat and rolled on his side, resting the Colt on his thigh so that it pointed down the length of the gully.

Minutes passed in dead silence. Then there was a sound; but not close or in the pines. It was the sound of horse's hoofs, distant, still far out on the meadow.

More of them, Cable thought.

He would have to take Vern quickly, before they came. He would have to keep it even if he expected to come through this.

And if you knew where Vern was maybe you could.

But he didn't. Vern could be close. Vern could even know he was lying here, and if he ran for the slope, Vern could very possibly drop him. Or even if he moved or stood up.

And if times if equals if, and there's no getting out of

this. No running. Only waiting and letting it happen. Even Forrest waited sometimes. He waited for them to make mistakes. But he would be waiting this time—God, yes, he would be waiting—whether they made mistakes or not.

The horse sound seemed nearer. He concentrated, listening, until he was sure that it was only one horse coming. One rider. One helper for Vern.

Cable pushed up with one hand, trying to see the meadow over the trees below him, but he could see only the far side of the meadow and the willows marking the river and the dark, quiet, cool-looking slope beyond. The rider would be close to this side by now.

Cable's gaze fell, and held.

Vern Kidston was facing him. Vern not thirty feet away, one leg in the gully, half sitting, half kneeling at the edge of it and partly hidden by the brush. Vern with his revolver extended and watching him.

Neither of them moved. They stared in silence with cocked revolvers pointed at each other. Cable sitting with one hand behind him, the other holding the Colt on his thigh, his face calm and showing clearly in the sunlight that filtered through the trees. Vern's expression, though partly shadowed and solemn with his mustache covering the corners of his mouth, was as relaxed as Cable's. The tension was somewhere between them, waiting for one or the other to move. And as the silence lengthened, it seemed that even a spoken word would pull a trigger.

It was in Vern's tone when finally he said, "Cable," and waited, as if expecting a reaction.

"I could have killed you," he said then. "I had my gun on you and you were looking away. . . . Why didn't I?"

Cable said nothing.

"I could have ended it right then. But I didn't. Do you know why?" He waited again. "I'm asking you."

Cable shook his head, though he saw Vern as he had seen him two days ago—a small figure against the front sight of his Spencer—and remembered how he had not been able to pull the trigger. He had thought about it enough and knew the reason why he had held back; but it was not a clear reason; only a feeling and it might be a different feeling with each man. What did Vern feel? At the same time, what difference did it make? Vern had not been able to pull the trigger when he had the chance, and knowing that was enough. But it would be different with him now, Cable thought, just as it's different with you. The feeling wouldn't apply or hold either of them back at this point.

Tell him anyway, Cable thought; and he said, "I had my sights on you once. The same thing happened. Though I'm not sure I'd let it happen again."

"When was that?"

"Two days ago. You were with Lorraine."

"Why didn't you shoot?"

"It takes some explaining," Cable said. "And I'm not sure it makes sense when you say it out loud."

Vern nodded faintly. "Maybe it's called leaving it up to the other man."

"I didn't start this," Cable said flatly. "I don't feel obliged to keep it going either."

"But you'll finish what you can," Vern said. "What about Austin—he's dead?"

Cable nodded.

"I didn't think you'd have a chance with him."

"Neither did he," Cable said. "That's why he's dead."

"So you killed all three of the Dodd brothers, and Royce—"

"What would you have done?"

"You mean because each time it was them or you?"

"Or my family," Cable said. "I'm asking what you would have done? Two choices. Run or stand?"

"All right." Vern paused. "But Duane. That's something else."

"I didn't shoot your brother."

"There's no one else would have reason to."

"Stay with one thing," Cable said. "I didn't shoot him."

"Even after he rawhided you?"

"If I'd wanted to get back at him for that, I'd have used fists. I never felt a beating was a killing thing."

"That could be true," Vern said. "But how do I know it is?"

"Whether you believe it or not," Cable answered,

"your gun's no bigger than mine is." But he said then, "I told you before, I didn't leave the house last night."

"And if you didn't do it—" Vern began.

"Why couldn't it have been one of your own men?"

Vern shook his head. "Everybody was accounted for."

Then it was Janroe, Cable thought, without any doubt of it. He said to Vern, "I can ask you the same kind of question."

"You mean about your house? I never touched it."

"Then it was Duane."

"I know for a fact," Vern said, "it wasn't anyone from my place."

"But you put Royce and Joe Bob on me."

Again Vern shook his head. "They came on their own."

"What about Lorraine?"

"I knew about that," Vern admitted. "I should have stopped her."

"What was the point of it?"

"Lorraine said wedge something between you and your wife. Split you up and you wouldn't have a good reason to stay here."

"Does that make sense to you?"

"I said I should have stopped her."

"Vern, I've lived here ten years. We've been married for eight."

Kidston nodded then, solemnly. "Bill Dancey said you had more reason to fight than I did."

"What did you say?"

"I don't remember."

"Do you believe him?"

"I'll tell you this," Vern said. "I'd like to have known you at a different time."

Cable nodded. "Maybe we would have gotten on. Even worked out this land thing."

"Even that," Vern said.

"I would have been willing to let you put some of your horses on my graze," Cable said, "if it hadn't started the way it did."

"Well, it doesn't matter now," Vern said.

But it could matter, Cable thought. "We were going

to wait each other out," Cable said. "But Royce and Joe Bob got into it. Then your brother. I wonder how this would have turned out if he were still alive."

Vern was watching Cable closely. "I wish I could understand you. Either you had nothing to do with killing Duane, or else you're some actor."

"Like trying to understand why you brought Wynn and Austin with you," Cable said. "You're big enough to make your own fight."

"When a man's killed," Vern said, "it's no longer a game or a personal contest. It was time to get you, with the best, surest way I had."

"When the man's your brother," Cable said. "When Royce and Joe Bob were killed you went right on waiting."

"I've been wrong," Vern said, "maybe right from the beginning. I let it get out of hand too. I admit that. But there's nothing I can do about the ways it's developed."

"Then in time you would have backed off," Cable said, "if nothing had happened to Duane."

"Well, with the war on I could look on you as an enemy. Kick you off your land and tell myself it was all right. But now that it's over, I'm not sure about anything, not even my horse business. Though I might probably get a contract from the stage-line people when they start up—"

Cable stopped him. "What did you say?" He was staring at Vern intently. "About the war?"

"It's over. You knew that, didn't you?"

"When was it over?"

"A few days ago."

"You knew it then?"

"We learned yesterday." Vern seemed to frown, studying Cable's expression. "Luz knew about it. She mentioned it when I talked to her a while ago."

"Yesterday," Cable said.

"She would have learned it yesterday." Vern nodded.

And if she knew it, Cable thought, so did Janroe. Yesterday. Before Duane was killed. Janroe would have known. He must have known. But still he killed Duane. Could that be?

You could think about it, Cable thought, and it

154

wouldn't make sense, but still it could be. With anyone else there would be a doubt. But with Janroe there was little room for doubt. This was strange because he hardly knew the man.

But at the same time it wasn't strange, not when he pictured this man who had lost his arm in the war and who had killed over a hundred Union prisoners. Not when he heard him talking again, insisting over and over that Vern and Duane should be killed. Not when he remembered the feeling of trying to answer Janroe. No, it wasn't strange, not when he put everything together that he could remember about Janroe.

It could have been Janroe who tore up his house. It occurred to Cable that moment, but at once he was sure of it: Janroe trying to incite him, trying to make him angry enough to go after the Kidstons. Janroe wanting to see them—the enemy, or whatever they were to him—dead, but without drawing blame on himself.

Janroe could even be insane. Something could have happened to him in the war.

No, don't start that, Cable thought. Just take it at its face value. Janroe killed a man you are being accused of killing. He did it, whether he had reason or not; though the war wasn't the reason, because the war was over and you are almost as sure as you can be sure of something that he knew it was over. So just take that, Cable thought, and do something with it.

He sat up, raising the Colt, then turned the cylinder, letting the hammer down gently on the empty chamber. Vern did not move; though when Cable looked up again he knew Vern had been taken by surprise and was puzzled.

"We're wasting our time," Cable said. "There's a man we ought to see."

He began to tell Vern about Janroe.

Luz reached Cable's dead sorrel before she saw the two horses grazing along the mesquite at the foot of the slope. These would belong to Vern and the one called Austin. She slowed the dun to a walk now, her eyes raised and moving searchingly over the piñon-covered slope. The firing had come from up there, she was sure of it.

But there had been no shots for some time now. They could be hunting for him among the trees. Or it could already be over.

When she saw the two figures coming down through the trees, in view for brief moments as they passed through clearings, she was sure that it was over, that these two were Vern and Austin coming back to their horses. They left the piñon and were down beyond the mesquite for sometime. Finally they appeared again and it was not until now that she saw the second man was not Austin but Cable.

She watched them approach with the strange feeling that this could not be happening, that it was a dream. They had been firing at one another; but now they were walking together, both armed, not one bringing the other as a prisoner.

Questions ran through her mind and she wanted to ask all of them at once; but now they were close and it was Cable who spoke first.

"Luz, did Janroe leave the store last night?"

The question took her by surprise. Without a greeting, without an explanation of the two of them together, without wondering why she was here, Cable asked about Janroe. The question must be so important to him that he skipped all of those other things.

She said, hesitantly, "He went to see you last night. But he said you weren't home."

"Where is he now, at the store?"

"He was a little while ago." She remembered him jumping down from the platform, trying to stop her from leaving. "But he's acting strangely," she said. "I don't think I've ever seen him the way he was."

Vern was looking at Cable. "Your wife and kids are there?" When Cable nodded, glancing at Luz again, Vern said, "I think we'd better go see Mr. Janroe."

Janroe watched Luz until she was almost out of sight. He turned, pausing to brush the dust from his knees, and was aware of Martha in the doorway. He looked up at her; from her expression he knew she had heard Luz.

"Well?" Janroe said.

"I would like to borrow a horse," Martha said tensely.

"You can't do anything."

"Just let me have a horse," Martha said. "I don't need anything else from you, least of all advice."

"And you'll take your kids with you?"

"I'd like to leave them here."

Janroe shook his head. "I don't have time to watch your kids."

Martha came out on the platform. "You would stop me from going to my husband? At a time like this you would stop me from being with him?"

"You couldn't help him," Janroe said. "Neither could I. Luz is wasting her time whether she thinks she's doing something or not. I tried to stop her, tried to talk some sense into her, but she wouldn't listen. That's the trouble with you women. You get all het up and run off without thinking." He had moved to the platform and was now mounting the steps. "If Vern's there to talk to your husband, there's no sense in stopping him. If he's there for any other reason, none of us could stop him if we tried."

"You won't let me have a horse?"

"Sit down on your hands, you won't be so nervous."

"Mr. Janroe, I'm begging you—"

"No, you're not." He moved her into the store in front of him. "You want to do something, get out in the kitchen and do the dishes."

Martha didn't want to back down—he could see that—but there was little she could say as she turned abruptly and walked away, down the length of the store counter.

Janroe said after her, "Don't leave the house. You hear me? Don't even open the door less I say it's all right."

He waited until she was in the next room before he moved around behind the counter that extended along the front of the store. From under the counter he took a short-barreled shotgun with *Hatch & Hodges* carved into the stock—it dated from the time the store had been a stage-line station—checked to see that it was loaded, then laid it on the counter.

From a peg behind him he took his shoulder holster

with the Colt fitting snugly in it, and looped it over his armless shoulder. He wound the extra-long leather thong, which held the Colt securely, around his chest and tied the end of it deftly with his one hand.

Just in case, he told himself; though you won't need them. You can be almost absolutely sure of that.

Everything will go all right. Luz would be back within an hour. She would ride in slowly this time, putting off telling Martha what had happened. Then behind her would come Vern and Austin, probably both of the Dodd brothers, with Cable face-down over his horse. Vern would tell it simply, in few words; and if Martha cried or screamed at him, he would say, "He killed my brother." Or, "He should have thought about his family before he killed Duane." Or words that said the same thing. Then they would dump his body. Or let it down easy now that it was over and the anger was drained out of them, and ride away.

Then what? Then he would listen to the woman cry, the woman and the kids. There was no way of avoiding that. Afterward, he might even offer his services to the new widow. . . .

Then what? Kill Vern? No, forget about that for now.

Then think about it when the time comes. There was no hurry. He could go back to St. Augustine. Or he could stay here. That would be something, to stay here and be a neighbor of Vern's. Talk to him about Duane every once in a while, and Cable, and all the trouble Cable caused. That would be something; but the staying here, the living here and letting the time pass, might not be worth it. He would have to weigh that against the once-in-a-while satisfaction of Vern talking to him and not knowing he had killed Duane.

No, there was no hurry. There would be time later on to think of what he would do. With two arms he would have stayed in the army; even though the war was over.

Janroe caught himself. Is it over?

All right, it's over. You've had no word, he thought. But if they want to say it's over, then it is. It was a good war, part of it was; but now, as of right now, you can say it's over. You can't fight people who won't fight back.

First Luz would come, then Vern. Everything had happened just about the way it was supposed to and there was no reason for it to change now.

Finding Luz gone this morning had affected his nerves. He knew she had gone to see Cable, and he had pictured her telling him that the war was over. Then asking him if he was at home last night. Then why, she would ask, would Janroe lie and say you weren't home? Then he had pictured Cable coming to the store.

But it had worked out all right. Vern was there before her. Vern seeking vengeance.

So now there was no chance of Cable finding out and eluding Vern or beating him or coming here. No, he would come here, all right, but not alive.

But this damn waiting . . .

Janroe paced the length of the space behind the counter, but it was too confining. He went out to the loading platform and for some time stood gazing out at the sunlit sweep of the valley; then at the willows and the slope beyond. He went inside again, through the store to the sitting room. From here he saw Martha still in the kitchen. Davis, the older boy, was with her, standing on a chair to put the breakfast dishes away.

He heard a noise from upstairs, then remembered that the other two children were up there. Martha had sent Clare up to make her bed and the younger one had gone with his sister. They'd probably forgotten all about the bed and were playing.

He was out on the platform again in time to see the rider come down the slope and drop from sight behind the willows. Waiting, Janroe was aware of the tight feeling in his stomach and the ache, the dull, muscle ache, in the arm that wasn't there. But the next moment the tension and the pain were gone. He could feel only relief now, watching Luz appear out of the willows and come toward him across the yard.

He saw her watching him as she came, all the way, until she had reached the platform.

"What happened?"

"It's over."

"He's dead?"

159

Luz glanced at the doorway behind them, then back to Janroe and nodded quickly.

"Where is he?"

"At home."

"I thought Vern would be coming."

Luz shrugged. "I don't know." She dismounted and came up on the platform. "I'd better go tell her."

Janroe stepped aside. "Go ahead." He said then, "You don't seem broken up any."

Luz said nothing.

"Didn't Vern say he was coming?"

Luz shook her head. "I don't remember." She moved past him into the store.

Janroe followed. "Wait a minute. Tell me what happened."

"After," Luz said. She hurried now to the next room.

Janroe still stood at the edge of the counter after she was gone.

But why wasn't she crying? She could be nervous about telling Martha, but she would have cried, if not now sometime before, and she would show signs of it.

From this the suspicion began to build in his mind. Why wouldn't she tell what happened? She seemed to want to get away from him, to see Martha too quickly; not holding back, putting it off, reluctant to face Martha; but wanting to see her, to tell her . . . to tell her what?

He moved through the store in long, hurried strides, across the sitting room and saw them in the kitchen, Martha and Luz and the little boy: Martha looking at him, her eyes alive and her hand going to Luz suddenly to stop her.

"What're you telling her?"

Luz turned, stepping back as he came in. "Nothing. I was just beginning—"

"What did she tell you?" He turned to Martha abruptly.

"This doesn't concern you, Mr. Janroe."

"Answer me!" His hand clamped on Martha's arm and he saw her wince, trying to pull away. "She said your husband was still alive, didn't she? She said not to worry that he was all right, that he was coming." Janroe shook her violently. "Answer me!"

160

He heard Luz moving. He wheeled, reaching for her, but she was already past him. "Luz—"

She ran through the store ahead of him, out to the loading platform and jumped. Janroe reached the doorway. He pulled the Colt, cocking it, and screamed her name again, a last warning. But beyond Luz he saw Cable step out of the willows with the Spencer in his hand. Then Vern, closer, running past the corner of the building. Janroe pushed back inside. He thought of Martha and ran into the sitting room in time to see her starting for the stairs. She reached the first step before she heard Janroe and turned to face him.

"You couldn't leave the two upstairs, could you?" Janroe said.

Now they were in the willows watching the front of the store. Vern had been down farther, in view of the rear door, but he had come back as Luz ran out of the store and Janroe shouted at her.

"That nails it down," Vern said. "He killed Duane. I wonder what he's thinking, seeing us together."

Cable, at the edge of the trees, said nothing.

Luz was staring vacantly at the adobe. "I shouldn't have run," she said. "I should be there with your wife and children."

"You did the best thing," Cable said.

"But I ran, leaving them alone with him."

"We shouldn't have let you do it," Cable said.

"No," Vern said. "It was the only way and it had to be tried. It was worth that much." The plan had been for Luz to tell Janroe that Cable was dead. Then to tell Martha, somehow without Janroe hearing, to take the children and slip out. That would leave Janroe alone in the adobe and in time they would take him. But now they would have to think of something else.

"Where was Martha?" Cable asked Luz.

"In the kitchen."

"The children with her?"

"Just Davis." She looked at him then. "Could Clare and Sandy be outside?"

"They'd be close. But I haven't seen them." He

glanced at Vern. "In back?" When Vern shook his head, Cable said, "Then they're all inside."

"He wouldn't harm them," Luz said. "He would be too afraid to do that."

"Now he'll be thinking of a way out," Vern said.

"Unless he's already thought of it." Cable was still watching the adobe. "I think I'd better talk to him."

Vern looked at him. "Just walk out there?"

"I don't know of any other way," Cable said. He parted the willow branches and started across the yard. Almost at once Janroe's voice stopped him.

"Stay where you are!"

Luz's horse, by the loading platform, raised its head at the sound.

Cable's eyes moved from the screen door to the first window on the right. One of the wooden shutters was open. If Janroe was there he would be in the store, behind the counter that ran along the front wall. Cable started toward the adobe again.

"Stand or I'll kill you!"

That's where he was, by the window. Cable was sure of it now.

"Janroe, you're in enough trouble. Let my family come out."

There was no answer from the store.

"You hear me? Send them out and nobody will harm you." He saw Janroe at the window then, part of his head and shoulder momentarily.

"How do I know that?" Janroe's voice again.

"You've got my word."

"I've got something better than your word."

"Janroe, if you harm my wife and children—"

"I'm through talking to you, Cable!"

"All right"—Cable's tone lowered, became more calm—"what do you want?"

"I'll tell you when I'm ready. Go back where you were. Try sneaking up and you'll hear a shotgun go off."

Cable stared at the window, not moving.

"Go on!"

"Janroe," Cable said finally, "if you harm my family you're a dead man." He turned then and moved back into the willows to stand with Luz and Vern.

Soon after, Luz's horse moved away from the platform, the reins dragging. It wandered aimlessly at first, nosing the ground; but finally the horse's head rose and it came toward them, drawn by the scent of water.

Taking the reins, Luz looked at Cable. "He could threaten us to bring it back. Why doesn't he?"

"He knows he can do it any time he wants," Cable answered.

They waited, watching the store and seldom speaking. The afternoon dragged by and there was no word from Janroe; not a sound reaching them from the adobe.

In the late afternoon, with the first red traces of sunset, a rider came down the slope from the horse trail south. It was Manuel, back from Hidalgo. Back for good, he said.

He looked at Vern, then at Cable inquiringly and Cable told it, beginning with Duane and bridging to the present time. They had been here nearly six hours now, waiting for Janroe to make his move. There was nothing they could do. There wasn't much doubt that Janroe would take a hostage when he decided to make his run. Probably one of the children. Probably, too, he was waiting for dark. But you couldn't count on anything—it was Luz who added this—because something was wrong with the man's mind. But Cable was sure Janroe would know they would hold back for fear of harming the child, and Janroe would lose them long before daylight.

The question then, what would he do with his hostage?

Cable said it bluntly, calmly, though his stomach was tight and he felt the unceasing urge through his body to move about and to do something with his hands. To do *something*.

It was Vern who brought up the question of the back door. "He can't watch front and back both. Unless he locked the door."

Manuel shook his head. "There's no lock on it. But what if he heard you?"

"That's something else," Vern said.

The evening came gradually with dusk filtering into the willow grove before seeping in long shadows out toward the adobe store. There were faint sounds of birds up in the ridge pines, but close about them the willows were silent. Later on, perhaps, there would be a breeze and the crickets would begin. But now there was a silence that seemed never to end. They waited.

Luz and Vern sat close to each other and occasionally Cable would hear the murmur of their voices. Janroe had split them apart and now he had brought them back together. Maybe they would get married. Maybe some good would come out of this. Later on—days or weeks, sometime later—he and Vern would talk this out that was between them. Cable remained apart from the others, sitting near the edge of the river and watching the dark water.

After a while he began to think of something Vern had said, about the back door. And Manuel had answered that there was no lock on the door. "But what if he heard you?" Manuel had asked.

But, Cable thought, what if he didn't hear you?

He pictured himself keeping to the trees until he had reached the barn, then creeping along its shadows, then across the yard and carefully, quietly, into the kitchen. It would already be dark inside the house. But if you bumped something—

No, he thought then, you know the place well enough. You could blind your eyes and walk through the house without touching or bumping anything.

Janroe wouldn't expect anyone and there would be no sound. Janroe would be by the window watching Martha and the children, but glancing outside often. He would creep to the doorway that led into the store, see Janroe and be very sure of killing him with the first shot.

An hour passed. It was dark in the willows now and the last red traces of sun were gone from the sky. Cable kneeled at the sandy edge of the river to drink, cupping the water in his hands.

In the other time, Martha would be getting the children ready for bed now. They would come in and kiss him good night before Martha sat with them on the bed, their eyes wide and watching her, while she told them a story.

There had been a story the children liked and asked for often, about the little girl and her brother who were lost in the forest. When night came, the little girl began to cry and her brother put his arm around her. They sat huddled together, shivering with cold and listening to the night sounds. And when it seemed they could bear no more, neither the cold nor the frightening sounds, the little girl's guardian angel appeared and led them through the forest to their home.

The children liked the story because it was easily imagined and because of the good feeling of being safely at home while they pictured themselves in the frightening dark.

Soon part of this story would come to life for one of his children. Janroe would take one of them as a hostage, because a child would be easier to handle than Martha. He would need only one horse and hold the child in front of him on the saddle, moving south toward the border and keeping to the wild terrain that offered good cover. But somewhere along the way, when he was sure he had lost the ones trailing him, when he no longer needed his hostage, Janroe would drop the child.

He would have no concern for the child's life. There was no reason even to hope that he might. It could be Sandy. Three years old and alone somewhere in the vast, trackless rock country to the south. If they didn't find him—and it would be almost as miraculous as the story if they did—the boy would survive perhaps two days.

So you have no choice, Cable thought. He would have to stop Janroe before he left the store.

Or while he was leaving it—

Cable pushed himself erect. Perhaps that was it. With the back door idea to make it work.

Perhaps as Janroe came out with the child in front of him. But it would be a long shot, too far, and even now there wasn't enough light. But say Vern worked his way around to the side of the adobe and waited there. That could be done.

Janroe would come out, would call for one of them to come unarmed with a horse, threatening to shoot the child if he wasn't obeyed. He would mount first and pull his hostage up in front of him. Or he would put the child up first. Either way, there would be a moment when Janroe would be seen apart from the child.

That was the time. You'll be there, Cable thought.

Through the store as he walks out, right behind him, and fire from the doorway, from close range.

But if the child was in the way then it would be Vern's shot. Vern shooting from about fifty feet, in the dark.

There was no other way.

When he presented his plan to the others there were objections; but finally, after talking it out and seeing no alternatives, they agreed to it. After that each of them thought about what he would do.

Martha sat on an empty packing case with her arm around Davis next to her. It was dark in the store with the night showing in the doorway and in the window behind Janroe. The counter separated them. On it, pointed at Martha and the boy, was the shotgun. It was within easy reach of Janroe sitting on a high stool with the Colt revolver in his hand.

Davis stirred, squirming on the wooden case, making it creak and causing Janroe to look at them. Martha's hand, with her arm around him, patted Davis gently. There was no sound from the other children now.

They were still locked in the upstairs bedroom and through the long afternoon Martha had listened to the faint sounds of their crying. Perhaps they were asleep now, even though they were frightened and had had nothing to eat since breakfast.

That seemed such a long time ago.

First Luz coming, riding in with the excitement on her face and talking to Janroe. Then returning, coming into the kitchen and telling her that it was over and that Cable was alive.

Then Janroe. She remembered the fear, the desperation in his eyes as he herded them upstairs, pushing them to make them hurry. He made Davis go into the bedroom where Clare and Sandy were playing; but as if something occurred to him, he brought Davis out and locked the door. He herded them downstairs again; closed the kitchen door and kicked at it angrily when he saw it had no lock. From the kitchen he moved them into the store, where they now sat.

When Cable came out of the trees and Janroe called

to him to halt, Martha stood up. She caught only a glimpse of her husband in the yard before Janroe ordered her to sit down. Once Cable's voice rose threateningly and Martha tensed, seeing the strained look of desperation come over Janroe's face again.

But as the morning stretched into afternoon, Janroe seemed to gain confidence. Gradually his expression became calm and he sat quietly on the stool, his movements, as he looked from the yard to Martha, less nervous and abrupt.

Martha noticed it. She watched him closely, noting each change in his manner as he became more sure of himself. Occasionally, as he looked outside, her eyes would drop to the shotgun on the counter. It was five feet away, no more than that; but it was pointed at her. It would have to be picked up and turned on Janroe; while all he had to do was raise his revolver a few inches and pull the trigger.

Twice she asked him what had happened, why he was holding them; but both times he refused to talk about it.

Janroe came off the stool when Luz's horse wandered from the platform to the trees. He stood at the window, his attention turned from Martha longer than at any time before. But finally he sat down again.

"My horse left me," Janroe said, looking at Martha. "But all I have to do is call and they'll bring it back." He seemed to be reassuring himself.

Martha watched him. "Then you're leaving?"

"In time."

"Alone?"

"Now wouldn't that be something."

"I didn't think so."

"Your boy's going with me."

Martha hesitated. "Will you take me instead?"

Janroe shook his head. "Him. He's big enough to hold on, little enough to be managed."

Martha felt Davis close to her. She glanced down at his hand in her lap, then at Janroe again. "What will you do to him?"

"That's up to him. Tell him if he cries or tries to run, I'll hurt him something awful." Janroe's eyes moved from the boy to Martha. "He's no good to me dead; least not while I'm getting away from here."

"And after that?"

Janroe shrugged. "I suppose I'll let him go."

"Knowing he'd be lost, and possibly never found?"

"Honey, I've got to look out for myself."

"If you leave him or harm him in any way," Martha said quietly, "my husband will kill you."

"If he finds me he'll try."

"He gave you his word," Martha said. "If you release us, he'll let you go."

"But will Vern?"

"At least talk to him again," Martha urged. "Tell him where you'll leave our boy."

"That would be like giving myself up."

They spoke only occasionally after that. Now the room was silent but for Davis's restless movement. Martha watched Janroe, seeing his heavy-boned profile against the dull gray light behind him.

She thought of Clare and Sandy upstairs and of Davis, not looking at him, but feeling his small body pressed close to her side. If Janroe left with him she might never see her son again. Janroe would sacrifice Davis, admitting it with an offhand shrug, to save his own life. Could that happen? Would God let something like that happen?

No, she thought, don't blame God.

Cabe had an idea about that. People, he said, blamed God for bad luck because they had to blame somebody. Some things you can do something about, and with God's help you can do it even better. But others you can't do anything about, so you wait and try not to worry or feel sorry for yourself.

Which was this?

You can do something, Martha thought. Because you have to do something.

Her eyes went to the shotgun. A dull, thin line of light extended from the breech to the blunt end of the barrel. Two steps to the counter, Martha thought. Her right hand would go to the trigger, raising the gun, swinging it on Janroe at the same time. Three seconds to do that. Four at the most. But it would take him only one.

Janroe turned from the window. "All right. Tell him he's going with me."

"You won't talk to my husband again? To Vern?"

"Tell him!"

She saw Janroe turn to the window again and call out, "Cable—send Luz over here with the horse!" He waited. "You hear me? Just Luz. If anybody else comes I'll kill your boy." His voice rose to a shout. "I mean it!"

Then it's now, Martha thought. She could feel her heart beating as she bent close to Davis and whispered to him. The boy started to speak, but she touched his mouth with the tips of her fingers, her own lips still close to his ear, telling him calmly, carefully, what he would have to do. The boy nodded and Martha kissed his cheek.

Janroe was looking at her again. "Is he ready?"

Martha nodded.

"As soon as she starts over with the horse, we go out to the platform."

Janroe's elbow rested on the window sill, his right shoulder against the side frame. The Colt in his hand was close to his body and pointed to just below the top of the counter.

When he moves it, Martha thought. The moment he turns.

Janroe looked out, but the Colt remained in the same position. Martha's gaze held on it. She heard him call out again, "Luz, bring the horse! You hear me? Luz—"

Janroe wheeled, seeing Martha already at the counter. She was less than four feet from him, raising the shotgun, turning it on him. He slashed out with the Colt, knocking the barrel aside as Martha's finger closed on one trigger. The blast was almost in his face and he struck the barrel again, lunging against the counter and turning Martha with the force of the blow.

"Janroe!"

Martha heard it—Cable's voice—and in the same moment saw Janroe's Colt swing toward the sound of it. Cable was in the doorway to the sitting room. He fired and Janroe stumbled against the wall. Cable fired again, but this shot smashed into the window frame. Janroe was already moving. He had been hit in the body, but he reached the doorway and lunged out to the platform.

Vern stepped away from the corner of the building. He fired three times, deliberately, taking his time, each shot finding Janroe, the last one toppling him from the edge of the platform.

Martha felt Cable move past her, past Davis, moving quickly but making almost no sound in his stockinged feet. She thought of the children upstairs.

"Davis, get Clare and Sandy."

She heard the boy run into the darkness of the next room before she turned and walked out to the platform to where Cable stood at the edge. Martha looked down, not seeing Janroe on the ground, but thinking of her children and her husband and wanting to be held.

The shotgun barrel slipped through her fingers until the stock touched the boards. She let it fall, feeling Cable's arm come around her.

ABOUT THE AUTHOR

ELMORE LEONARD has written over fifteen novels and numerous short stories, several of which have been turned into successful films including *3:10 to Yuma* and *Valdez Is Coming*. He has also written the screenplays for such films as *Joe Kidd*, starring Clint Eastwood, and *Mr. Majestyk*, starring Charles Bronson. His novel, *Hombre*, was chosen as one of the twenty-five best Western novels ever written by the Western Writers of America and *The Switch*, published by Bantam, was nominated by the Mystery Writers of America for the Edgar Allan Poe Award for the best paperback of 1978.

Of his interest in the West, Mr. Leonard writes: "At the rail of a Missouri River steamboat Gary Cooper sees, for the first time, a man smoking a cigarette. He comments, 'Mister, your toothpick's on fire.' And before *The Plainsman* was over—and Porter Hall, the cigarette smoker, had shot Cooper in the back—I was hooked on Westerns forever. More inspiration came from *My Darling Clementine* and *Red River*. And finally, a year after *The Gunfighter* appeared, I was writing them myself. Curiously though, I'm inspired and motivated more by a novel that isn't a Western—though it seems to have the basic elements—than by traditional Western novels and motion pictures; and that's Hemingway's *For Whom The Bell Tolls*. But maybe it isn't so strange. The desire to write or read Westerns comes more from a feeling than a visual stimulus. Living in Detroit, as I do, wouldn't seem to be conducive. There sure aren't any buttes or barrancas out the window. But if you squint hard enough—wherever you are—you can see riders coming with Winchesters and Colt revolvers, and watch them play their epic roles in a time that will never die."

A Special Preview of
the powerful opening pages of Volume 5
in the bestselling Wagons West series

TEXAS!
by
Dana Fuller Ross

Here is the long-awaited new volume in the
series begun with INDEPENDENCE, NE-
BRASKA, WYOMING, and OREGON.
TEXAS continues the adventures of Lee and
Cathy Blake, Whip Holt and other wagon train
members as they join together again to brave
many new dangers and save another territory
for our growing nation.

I

Captain Rick Miller, head of the criminal investigation division of the Texas Rangers, rode at a seemingly easy canter across the vast plains of the young Republic. Homesteaders whom he passed as they worked in their fields and with whom he exchanged friendly waves, wouldn't have guessed that two of his Rangers, following behind him, were hard pressed to maintain his pace.

Tall and sinewy, with a physical strength and endurance that his slender frame did not indicate, Rick kept a constant watch in all directions, his pale eyes squinting beneath the blazing, shadeless sun. For six months the authorities had been unable to capture a gang of thieves that preyed on isolated farms and ranches. The day before, when a report had been received in Austin regarding the area in which the criminals were now operating, the task of killing or capturing them had been given to Captain Miller. Respecting the power of the pistol hanging from a holster at his belt and the rifle slung from his shoulder, Rick believed in shooting only when necessary, but at the same time was sworn to rid Texas of lawbreakers, and President Sam Houston himself had said, "I'd hate to have Rick Miller on my trail."

Although he didn't want to admit it to himself, Rick was pleased he had the opportunity to leave Austin—with its grubby murders and robberies that were commonplace in a new civilization—and return for a time to the field. He loved the open spaces as much as he despised criminals.

One of these years, he reflected, he would leave

the Rangers, find some property he liked, and settle down. He was in no great rush, to be sure. A man needed a wife for that kind of life. At the moment there was no woman who interested him, and, he had to admit, he was more than a little uncomfortable in the presence of ladies. The only women he had ever known since the death of his parents had forced him to go out into the world on his own, had been harlots, and his relations with them had been brief and cursory. He attended to his physical needs, then went on his way.

Looking back, he took pride in the knowledge that he had come a long way since the death of his parents and his start in the Rocky Mountains where he had lived for years as a trapper and hunter before migrating to Texas, where he had become a Ranger almost immediately. He had been wise to give up the life of a mountain man, which offered few opportunities these days. The great heroes of the Rockies were gone now. Jim Bridger had set up a trading post somewhere in the mountains, either in the Utah or Wyoming countries, and Kit Carson, the last he had heard, was in California. Sam Brentwood had become completely civilized and lived with his wife and family in Independence, Missouri, where he owned a supply depot that provided essentials for members of wagon trains heading westward. Even Rick's own hero, Whip Holt, had married and remained in Oregon after leading the first wagon train to that territory.

Smiling slightly, Rick shook his head. It was hard to think of Whip Holt as a married man. He guessed he himself could be tamed, too, if the right woman ever came into his life, but he shrank from the thought. He was too independent. And, he had to concede, assignments like his present job still gave him a feeling that he was performing a genuine service. He was not ready to settle down.

A cloud of dust on the horizon caught Rick's attention. "Look yonder," he called to his two Rangers, and instantly he increased his pace to a full gallop.

His men did the same, silently cursing him. While

it was true that Captain Miller had become famous because of his instinct for smelling trouble, they saw no need to exert themselves unduly on what well might be a wild-goose chase.

Rick's stallion responded to the slight touch of his spurs and ran steadily, his hoofs thundering on the hard, dry ground beneath his feet. It hadn't rained in weeks, much to the distress of the plains farmers, but a horse could make better time on such ground.

A farmhouse came into view in the distance, with two barns behind it, and when Rick made out five horses tied to hitching posts near the front door, he became even more alert. Signaling to the Rangers behind him to follow his example, he unslung his rifle, made sure it was ready for instant use, and cocked it.

An unseen woman's scream sounded from somewhere behind the house and was followed by a single shot. Then all was silent again.

Before Rick and his men could reach the house, five men, all armed, raced around to the front of the house, four of them carrying filled burlap sacks.

Rick and the Rangers had two choices; either they could dismount and shield themselves behind their horses, or they could continue to ride forward, taking a greater risk, relying on their momentum to achieve a victory in the face of odds that were almost two to one against them. Rick chose the latter course.

The man who was not carrying a burlap sack appeared to be the leader, and as he reached for his pistol, Rick instantly drew a bead on him with his rifle and squeezed the trigger. So certain of his aim that he reloaded without delay while still riding, a feat that few could emulate, Rick had the satisfaction of seeing the man crumple to the ground, a small, neat hole in the center of his forehead.

The Rangers fired a second or two later. One bullet found its mark, and another man fell to the ground, flinging his arms upward and dropping his burlap sack with a crash as he died. The other Ranger missed his target completely, but now the odds were even. Rick fired a second shot as quickly as he could raise his rifle to his shoulder, and again he was successful.

By now the two remaining thieves had placed their burdens on the ground and were returning the Rangers' fire with their own pistols. A bullet whistled past Rick's head, close to his ear, but he did not flinch. Instead he felt angry. Timing his move carefully, he forced his superbly trained stallion to a halt, at the same time leaping to the ground and firing his pistol at one of the remaining pair before they had the chance to reload. For the third time he found his target.

The last of the robbers turned and started to run. Rick had no opportunity to reload now, but he sprinted after the criminal. Using his rifle as a club, he grasped the weapon by its still warm barrel and sent the stock smashing into the side of the man's head. Blood spurted from his head as he dropped like a felled log and lay motionless, his sightless eyes fixed on the pale, cloudless sky.

The two Rangers were not surprised at their superior's accomplishments. Dispatching four of their five foes had been a typical Rick Miller performance.

Leaving the Rangers to make certain that all five of the criminals were indeed dead, Rick walked to the rear of the house, then removed his hat when he saw the tableau that awaited him. A man with the tanned face and forearms of one who lived behind a plow was stretched on the ground, a faint trickle of blood still oozing from the spot on his chest where a thief's bullet had killed him. Standing over him, dry-eyed, was a woman with a lined, careworn face and two girls in their early teens, who wept as they clung to their mother.

"Miller, Texas Rangers, ma'am," Rick called, announcing himself so he would not alarm the trio.

The woman looked at him and nodded, her face blank.

"I'm afraid we got here too late, but those thieves won't do any more damage, not to anybody," he said.

"Thank God for that much," she replied in a dry, cracked voice.

He moved a few steps closer, then halted, feeling very much ill at ease. He had no idea that, when he spoke again, there was genuine compassion, even a touch of tenderness, in his voice. "We'll return your stolen property to the house for you, ma'am, and we'll remove the bodies of those bobcats so you won't have to look at them again. Is there anything else we can do for you?"

"Yes, please." Like so many who lived on the frontier, the newly widowed woman was eminently practical, even in a time of great tragedy. "I'll be obliged to you if you'll dig a grave for my husband's body. The girls and I have no heart for it."

"Yes, ma'am," he murmured.

"You'll find shovels in the near barn," she said, then led her children into the house.

Rick and his Rangers went to work digging a grave, fashioning a crude coffin, dragging the bodies of the thieves off the property, and throwing them into a gully, where the vultures soon would dispose of their remains, and then piling the stolen goods on the front porch. Rick noted absently that it was in need of paint.

There were several other chores that had to be done, and then Rick tapped at the door. The woman, still dry-eyed, opened it and stood on the threshold.

"It won't make up for the loss of your husband, ma'am, but I've put the thieves' horses in the big barn for you. I reckon you can get a fairly good price for them. They're all sound geldings. And here are the robbers' firearms, along with a purse that's filled with all the money they were carrying. Maybe all this will help tide you over."

An expression of gratitude appeared in her shocked, grief-stricken eyes. He became still more uneasy. If there was anything that upset him, it was being thanked for doing his duty. It didn't occur to him that he was going far beyond the call of duty, any more than he knew his voice and manner suggested a surprising inner, gentle quality that was at odds with his conduct when he tracked down criminals. He would have been astonished had anyone told him that he was a truly gentle man.

"What more can we do for you, ma'am?"

The woman hesitated for an instant, then said, "Would it be asking too much to bury my husband, please? My girls are taking it bad, but they'll accept his death as final once he's buried and they realize life must go on. That's why I hate to wait a day or so until the neighbors can gather."

As Rick well knew, the closest neighbors might live as far as five miles away. "It's the very least we can do," he said.

Again she hesitated. "Maybe you could read a prayer? I can fetch a Bible for you."

He had never read aloud, but duty sometimes made it necessary for a Ranger officer to do unusual things. "Is there something in particular you want me to read?"

She shook her head. "You choose it."

"Then," he replied, surprising himself as well as the widow, "I won't need the Bible."

A few minutes later the little group assembled behind the barn where the grave had been dug. The Rangers carried the farmer's coffin there and, at the widow's request, nailed it shut before her daughters came out of the house.

Rick knew without being told that she wanted the girls to remember their father as he had been in life. The woman called to her daughters, and when they joined her, she placed her arms around their shoulders.

Rick's instinct told him what to recite. He had been reared in a God-fearing home before the untimely death of his parents, and although he never spoke of his religion, his faith ran deep. His voice resonant but soft, he spoke the Twenty-third Psalm from memory.

At a nod from their commander the Rangers lowered the coffin into the ground and began to fill the excavation. One of the girls sobbed, and for the first time tears trickled down the woman's cheeks. She brushed them away. "That was beautiful." Her voice became firm as she issued an order. "Mr. Miller, you and these boys will stay to dinner."

Rick became fidgety. "We can't impose on you, ma'am."

"Stuff and nonsense, Mr. Miller," she said. "Dinner has been on the stove for hours, and if you don't eat it, I'll have to throw it out. If there's anything that's a sin, it's wasting good food when there are folks starving all over the world!"

It would be an insult to refuse her hospitality, so he agreed to stay.

An enormous bowl of beef stew was placed on the kitchen table, and with it the widow served a large loaf of crusty, hot bread and slabs of butter. The two young Rangers ate lustily, and the teen-age girls recovered sufficiently to engage them in conversation.

Rick had little appetite and pushed the stew around on his plate. He could not rid himself of the thought that he was eating a meal that had been intended for a man who was now dead. It was absurd, he reflected, for someone in his type of work to be so sensitive, and he wished he could curb his feelings sufficiently to live up to the hard-bitten image he presented to others.

"I'll drop in to see you whenever I'm out this way," he said at last. "And if there's anything you want or need, just send word to me at headquarters. I'll either come myself, or, if I'm too busy, I'll send one of the boys."

"That's right kind of you, sir," the widow replied. "As it happens, my son is due home in a month or two, so I reckon we can make out until then."

Rick was relieved. "How old is your son?"

"Twenty-three."

"Ah, then he's plenty old enough to do a man's work on your property. I was going to suggest that I could help find a hired hand for you."

"Oh, he's worked on the farm with his pa ever since he was a tyke, so he knows what needs to be done here. He just went off to St. Louis to pick up some new-fangled wheat and onion bulbs that are supposed to stay alive during the dry spells here." She paused, then looked at him carefully. "Are you always this helpful to the survivors of folks who are killed by thieves, Mr. Miller?"

He felt color rising to his face, and hoped it would not show beneath his heavy tan. "Well, ma'am," he said, "there's nothing in Ranger regulations that requires it. But the way I see things, Texas is putting up one whale of a fight for her existence. Between the weather and the threat of a new war with the Mexicans, who'll slaughter every last one of us if they win, we've got to stand together. It's the only way we'll survive." The discussion made him uncomfortable, so he turned to the two Rangers and issued a brusque order. "Help the youngsters clear away and wash the dishes, and we'll be on our way. We can reach Austin by late tonight if we push ourselves."

A few minutes later the widow escorted him to the front door, putting her hand on his arm for an instant. "Mr. Miller," she said quietly, "I want you to give your wife a message for me. Tell her she's a very lucky woman."

The embarrassed Rick didn't have the heart to tell her he was a bachelor.

He took the lead on the ride back across the open fields, his stallion settling into his customary canter. With his broad-brimmed hat shielding his pale eyes, his rifle and pistol ready for immediate use in case of need, Rick Miller looked, once again, like a tough-minded law enforcement officer.

Cathy Blake tried to achieve a more matronly appearance by fixing her long, blonde hair in a bun at the nape of her neck, but the effort failed. Standing by the window of the commandant's house at the Oregon fort overlooking the Columbia River, she looked as young and pretty as she had before her marriage, when she had driven her lead wagon in the first train that had crossed the continent. She glanced at her two-year-old daughter, Beth, who was sitting on the floor, busily scribbling on scratch paper, then resumed her vigil. Her husband was due home at any moment.

She saw him when he left his office and started across the parade ground, trim and erect in the blue uniform of a full colonel in the United States Army, his physique lithe, his step light. It was absurd after being a married woman for years, Cathy thought, to feel a warm glow when she saw her husband. Perhaps she was an incurable romantic, something she had never suspected about herself . . .

Lee came into the house, embraced his wife, and sat in his chair. Something was on his mind. "You've heard me speak of Colonel Bill Hawkins, my classmate at the military academy. We were roommates then, and we're still quite close."

"You correspond with him."

"Right. I had a letter from him today that was squeezed into the official pouch the War Department sent to me. Bill can get away with stunts like that because he's head of the Military Secretariat." He reached into an inner tunic pocket, removed a letter, and unfolded it. "Maybe I'd better interpret it for you."

"In spite of any opinions to the contrary held by the male member of this family—no name allowed, mind you—I am capable of reading simple English."

Lee chuckled and handed her the communication. "Help yourself."

Cathy studied the letter at length, frowning, then handed it back to him. "This is pure gibberish. Not one sentence makes sense."

"When there are very private matters to be discussed," he said, "Bill and I always use a code we once worked out when we were on an intelligence assignment together. Any snooping War Department clerk who might have opened the letter wouldn't have understood a word. As I said, Madame Wise One, I'll interpret for you."

"I not only stand corrected, but I'm ready to jump out of my skin."

"Please don't. I've never touched smoother, softer skin."

She couldn't help giggling. "Vulgar."

"Accurate," he countered, then became serious. "Because of his official position, Bill is privy to all sorts of inside War Department information before anyone else knows about it. The gist of this letter is to tell me that there's a transfer in store for me."

"Oh." She caught her breath and tried not to appear too concerned.

"All Bill can tell me about it is that something big is in store for me. Winnie—General Winfield Scott, the Chief of Staff—has had several discussions with President Tyler about it. At the moment everything is being kept secret, but Bill says I should get an official communication before long."

"How long is that?"

He shrugged. "Your guess is as good as mine."

"Colonel Hawkins has no idea what might be in store for you?"

"Apparently not, unless the post is so sensitive that he didn't want to be the one to break the news to me informally. All I can say for certain is that it won't be a routine transfer to the command of a garrison in the Nebraska country or New England or the South."

Cathy listened carefully. She loved Oregon and her friends whom she had met and grown close to on the wagon train. Yet she had known long before she married Lee, that no army assignment was permanent and that the day would come when they would be obliged to move.

"I've been thinking of every possibility. It could

be that a new Indian war is going to break out some-where."

"The Choctaw?"

"Not likely," he replied, grinning. "Andy Jackson taught them a lesson back when you were about Beth's age, and they haven't forgotten it. The puzzling angle of this thing is that Bill is sure I'll be able to take a few of my present people with me, like Sergeant Major Mullins. So I'd say that an Indian war is a strong pos-sibility. Another is a post in Texas."

"The United States isn't sending troops into the Republic of Texas! That would mean war with Mexico, wouldn't it, Lee?"

"That would be my hunch, but I don't have the information that's available to President Tyler, the State Department, and the War Department." He reached for a pipe from the rack beside him, then filled it slowly and carefully, an indication that he was deep in thought.

"Why should Texas be so important to the United States?"

"The situation is simple, fortunately or unfortu-nately. Our country has a legitimate claim to the Ore-gon country, as you well know, but so does Great Britain. We've avoided an armed conflict here. So far. And it's my hope, as it is that of the British garrison at Fort Vancouver across the Columbia, that the dispute will be settled by diplomatic means. Texas is a different kettle of fish."

"In what way?"

"Hear me out," he said patiently, always im-pressed and pleased by her eagerness to learn. "Texas is a vast country, and was virtually uninhabited for years. It was a province of Mexico, but very few Mexicans lived there. Americans are thrusting west-ward in great numbers, and have been for a number of years now. Naturally, there were thousands who were attracted—and are still attracted—by the fertile land in Texas that was going to waste. So Americans migrated there in large numbers—and are still migrating."

"I know part of the rest of the story," Cathy said. "General Santa Anna, the President of Mexico, gave the Americans in Texas a hard time."

"Yes, it was very rough for them. Santa Anna is a tyrant, a dictator. So the Americans rebelled, and Sam Houston, who was Governor of Tennessee a number of years ago, won the great Battle of San Jacinto from Santa Anna. Texas became an independent country."

"Of course. But why are we becoming involved?"

"Because American citizens are still moving to Texas in huge numbers. The migration there is even greater than it is to Oregon. The day is bound to come soon when Texas will become an American state. They want it. We want it."

"But Santa Anna doesn't want us to become stronger at what he believes is his expense."

"Precisely," Lee said. "I'm talking about a factual situation that exists, not the ethical question of whether it's right or wrong for Texas to break away from Mexico and ultimately become part of the United States. The Texans will go to war to protect their liberty, and we'll do the same."

"That," Cathy said, "is the part that confuses me."

"Santa Anna," Lee said, puffing hard on his pipe and momentarily obscuring his face in a cloud of blue smoke, "is a no-good, vindictive devil. If he should regain control of Texas, he'd execute or imprison and torture every man who took up arms against him. He's said as much in so many words, which is why the opposition to him in Texas is so great."

"I can imagine what would happen to the American women and children."

"Texans who lived under Santa Anna's rule don't have to imagine anything," he said bluntly. "They know."

"And you think you may be given command of a regiment in a new war in Texas?"

"I honestly don't know what to think, which is why I'm whirling, Cathy." He picked up the letter again and tapped it with the stem of his pipe. "Now we come to the core of our personal situation. Bill Hawkins was very clear and very emphatic about one thing. He swears I'll be able to take my family with me on my new assignment."

She sighed deeply, and then a smile of relief and joy spread slowly across her face. "Hallelujah! As long as you and I are going to be together, I don't care where you're transferred."

Rick Miller (an important new character), whose burning desire is to see Texas become part of the Union, is sent to Oregon in one phase of a daring plan created by Sam Houston. Also caught up in this campaign is Lee Blake, as well as his family, who must ultimately come to the defense of the Texas territory.

(Now read the complete Bantam Book, available September 1st wherever paperbacks are sold.)

"REACH FOR THE SKY!"

and you still won't find more excitement or more thrills than you get in Bantam's slam-bang, action-packed westerns! Here's a roundup of fast-reading stories by some of America's greatest western writers:

☐	14823	**THE PROVING TRAIL** Louis L'Amour	$1.95
☐	13651	**THE STRONG SHALL LIVE**	$1.95
☐	13781	**THE IRON MARSHAL**	$1.95
☐	14219	**OVER ON THE DRY SIDE** Louis L'Armour	$1.95
☐	13719	**RADIGAN** Louis L'Amour	$1.95
☐	14207	**THE WARRIOR'S PATH** Louis L'Amour	$1.95
☐	12378	**THE WHIP** Luke Short	$1.50
☐	13759	**THE TOUGH TEXAN** Will Cook	$1.75
☐	12888	**GUNSIGHTS** Elmore Leonard	$1.50
☐	14176	**FEUD AT SINGLE SHOT** Luke Short	$1.75
☐	14236	**THE BEAR PAW HORSES** Will Henry	$1.75
☐	12374	**ROYAL GORGE** Pete Dawson	$1.50
☐	13923	**GUNMAN BRAND** Thomas Thompson	$1.50
☐	08773	**THIS GUN IS STILL** Frank Gruber	$1.50
☐	12978	**WARBONNET** Clay Fisher	$1.50

Buy them at your local bookstore or use this handy coupon for ordering